CONNOR'S WAR

A Novel by
Greg Stout

For information, or to order additional copies, please contact:

Beacon Publishing Group
P.O. Box 41573 Charleston, S.C. 29423
800.817.8480| beaconpublishinggroup.com

Publisher's catalog available by request.

ISBN-13: 978-1-949472-53-0

ISBN-10: 1-949472-53-0

Published in 2022. New York, NY 10001.

First Edition. Printed in the USA.

ACKNOWLEDGMENTS

I would like to express my gratitude to several individuals who helped make this book possible, including friends Barbara Barbre and Bill Wade, as well as my wife, Carol, who assisted in proofreading and critiquing the content. You guys made this a better book that I ever would have been able to accomplish on my own. In addition, my very special thanks go to Captain Charlie Plumb, USN, himself a former Vietnam-era POW, and the author of *I'm No Hero*, a harrowing account of his six years in captivity, who generously gave his time to help me get the details right. Charlie, without question, you are a hero. Finally, sincere thanks to my editor, Bobby Collins, at Beacon Publishing Group, for his support in guiding this book on its journey from manuscript to published volume.

AUTHOR'S NOTE

Readers familiar with the towns and landscape of both the Central Valley of California and south-central Kansas will recognize that I have taken more than a few liberties with the description and details of both. This was entirely intentional, to fit the requirements of the story. In one or two instances, I have used the names of real people, always being careful to represent them in a favorable light. This book, like *Gideon's Ghost*, which preceded it, is strongly influenced by my tenure as a teacher for more than a decade and is for that audience that this book is intended. In my experience, young adults are among the smartest and most perceptive people anywhere, capable of asking the best questions and recognizing honest answers when they hear them.

CONNOR'S WAR

Greg Stout

PROLOGUE

The story begins this way.

On April 24, 1968, the United States Navy aircraft carrier *Constellation* sailed out of Subic Bay, an American naval base located in the Republic of the Philippines. A few days later, the *Constellation* arrived off the coast of North Vietnam at a point in the Gulf of Tonkin identified by U. S. military planners as Yankee Station. Beginning on the first day of May, U. S. Navy strike teams began bombing raids against the North Vietnamese port of Haiphong, mostly flying Grumman A-6 Intruder bombers protected by F4 Phantom fighter-bombers

The F4s were built by McDonnell Aircraft in St. Louis, Missouri. They were regarded as the most capable and formidable aircraft of their kind throughout the Vietnam War. An F4 could carry an ordnance payload of 18,000 pounds, and was capable of flying 1,473 miles per hour, or about twice the speed of sound. The flight crew of a Phantom consisted of two officers: the pilot, who was the flight commander, and a flight officer, who was responsible for navigation, communications and target acquisition—in other words, weapons.

On May 4, 1968, the *Constellation* launched a strike team which consisted of sixteen Intruders protected by eight F4s which served as flak suppressors, and another eight F4s whose task was MIG-CAPs, or combat air patrol to ward off counterattacks from Russian-built MIG fighters flown by North Vietnamese pilots. Flying at altitudes ranging from Angel 9 to Angel 11 (9,000 to 11,000 feet), the team's mission was to destroy targets along the 20th parallel, the site of numerous oil storage facilities in North Vietnam. That country had been under repeated air attack by American warplanes since early 1965 as part of Operation Rolling Thunder, the code name for a campaign of continuous raids initiated, as some said, to "bomb North Vietnam back into the Stone Age" and bring about the end of the war.

The area designated for attack on May 4 had been under bombardment since shortly after the Tet Offensive that took place in January 1968. During the raid, the strike team encountered typically heavy resistance, including anti-aircraft gunfire and SAMs, or surface-to-air, missiles. During the raid on that day, two of the Phantoms were hit. One was able to make it back to friendly air space in South Vietnam before setting safely down at Da Nang Air Base. The other plane was too badly damaged to remain in the air. The crew, including the pilot and his "back seat," flight officer Ensign Gerald Taney, were forced to eject over North Vietnamese-held territory near the DMZ, or demilitarized zone, the border area between North and South Vietnam. The fate of the flight crew was not immediately known, so the official record initially listed both men as MIA, or missing in action.

My name is Connor Ward. The officer in command of the plane that went missing on that day, Lieutenant Commander Richard Ward, is my father.

CHAPTER ONE

The day after my father's plane was lost, I pitched two innings in relief in a ninth-grade junior varsity baseball game against Tokay Junior High, a conference rival from nearby Madera, California. It wasn't a particularly important game. Our team had a mediocre 7-6 record going in. Tokay was 5-8, so neither of us had a shot at the conference championship. Even so, it felt good to win the final game of the year, and better still that I had gotten a save to help nail down the victory.

After the game and the usual stop for ice cream, I hitched a ride home from Bobby Sachs, our shortstop, and his dad, who had showed up to watch the last few innings of the game. Bobby's dad was a fireman for the city of Fresno, the city where we lived, and since this was one of his off-days, he was able to come and watch us play.

"You looked pretty good out there today, Connor," Mr. Sachs said on the ride home. "You threw two solid innings of shutout ball. That'll show up huge in tomorrow's box score."

"The school newspaper doesn't print a box score, Dad," Bobby said. "Nobody cares about the JV games. We'll be lucky if anybody except the other guys on the team even knows we played."

"That sucks for you, Bobby," I said. "That means Vicky won't know you were a major standout with three hits and no errors. That is, unless, you go bragging to her, and I know you'd never do a thing like that."

I was teasing him a little with that. Bobby had a crush a mile wide on Vicky Esposito, the prettiest girl in our class, and I knew he'd be on the phone to her with a play-by-play retelling of his heroics as soon as he got home.

"Well," Mr. Sachs said as he pulled into our driveway, "even without making the front page of the newspaper, it's good to end the season with a winning record. Makes you look forward to next year when you guys will be playing for the varsity."

He was right. It did feel good, and I was hoping to make varsity next spring. And I knew I would barely be able to wait until Dad called so I could tell him how we did. But I had no way of knowing at the time how long it would be before I got that call.

CHAPTER TWO

After I thanked Mr. Sachs for the ride home and exchanged "see you tomorrows" with Bobby, I picked up the newspaper from the driveway, collected the mail from the mailbox and let myself into the house. My mother was in the kitchen getting dinner ready.

"How did your game go?" she called over running water in the kitchen sink.

"Great," I said. I pitched the last two innings, struck out two and gave up one hit. We won 7-3."

Mom gave me a smile. "No doubt the Dodgers and the Giants will be knocking at our door any day now."

"Sure, they will. Maybe the Angels and the A's, too, if they decide to stay in Oakland. All I need to do now is learn how to throw a curveball," I said. "Did Dad call today?"

"No, but it's already close to midnight where he is. If he flew a mission, we probably won't hear from him until tomorrow."

I put the mail down on the kitchen counter where Mom could look through it when her hands were free.

"Right, I keep forgetting about the time

difference," I said, and headed down the hall to grab a shower before supper.

Like my father, my mom, Madeline Ward, was a United States naval officer, a lieutenant commander and a medical doctor. She and Dad were based stateside at Lemoore Naval Air Station. We lived in a rented house just outside Fresno, California, not far from Lemoore NAS. I attended Huntington Junior High School, also located in Fresno. In another two weeks, my ninth-grade school year would be over and summer vacation would begin. In the fall I would be moving on to Central Valley High School. My plan was to go out for track in the fall and then baseball in the spring. I thought I had a pretty good chance to make both teams. I was pretty fast around the bases, and sometimes, if I wasn't going to be pitching, the coach would put me in as a pinch-runner.

I had just finished toweling off and getting into jeans and a t-shirt when the doorbell rang.

"Could you get that, honey?" Mom said. "I'm up to my elbows in this meatloaf."

When I opened the door, there were two naval officers, a man and a woman, waiting on the porch, dressed in their service dress blue, or SBD, uniforms. The man wore the insignia of a captain, with four gold stripes on his epaulets and an eagle insignia on his collar. The woman was a lieutenant commander, same as my mother, with three gold stripes and a gold cross on her collar. That made her a chaplain.

In the seconds after I opened the door and saw the two officers standing on the front porch, it was as if my heart had stopped beating and my lungs stopped working. I had seen officers like this before, at another home in our neighborhood where a Marine officer's family lived. They were a notification detail. And they were about to give us some very bad news.

At the same moment I opened the door my mother looked out from the kitchen. She started to say, "Who is it, Con . . .," and that was as far as she got before the bowl she was using to mix the meat and the other ingredients for the meat loaf fell from her hands and crashed into pieces on the kitchen floor.

****

"Several of the remaining flight crews in the air saw Lieutenant Commander Ward and Ensign Taney eject, so we know they didn't go down with their aircraft." The officer speaking had introduced himself as Captain Robert Reynolds. When a notification detail is dispatched, at least one of the officers is always senior to the officer or seaman who has been lost. The other officer, Lieutenant Commander Mariel Salazar, was assigned to the detail to handle any religious or spiritual issues that might arise during the notification.

Captain Reynolds continued, "At this point, we are calling Lieutenant Commander Ward missing in action. We don't know if he and Ensign Taney were taken prisoner by North Vietnamese or Viet Cong forces, or if they managed to evade capture and find refuge in the countryside. For the moment, we're operating on the assumption that both officers survived. We've already notified both the Swedish and the Swiss consulates in Hanoi as well as the Red Cross and asked their people to follow up to do whatever they can to determine whether either or both men have become prisoners of war."

Captain Reynolds looked at Mom. "Do you have any questions so far?"

"How long?" she asked. Her voice was totally flat and emotionless, as if she were asking the most unimportant question anyone had ever posed.

"You mean until we know something more?" Captain Reynolds shook his head. "Doctor Ward, you know the situation. The North Vietnamese don't abide by the Geneva Convention, and they don't permit Red Cross visits to their prisoners of war, so it could be weeks or even months before we find out anything more. Maybe longer. For the moment, all we can do is hope for the best. I must tell you, though, that at the time the crew bailed out, they were over some very rugged and remote territory, so it's anybody's guess whether they'll be able to sustain themselves long enough to get back to freedom, especially if either one of them was injured after they ejected. Plus, if they were captured, and we have no way of knowing if they were, it can take weeks or even months before they finally wind up in a secure camp."

Mom and I both knew that already. There were plenty of families living near us who had lost pilots and ground troops in Vietnam. Marine infantrymen killed in combat were usually recovered by their brothers in arms, other soldiers who had gone into a firefight with them and then brought them back afterward. At the same time, it was not unusual for downed air crews to be rescued by recovery teams in low-flying helicopters within a day or two after being shot down, as long as they could remain hidden until help arrived. For the time being, at least, we had that hope.

Lieutenant Commander Salazar looked at me. "Connor? Your name is Connor, right?"

"Yes, ma'am," I said. In the military, officers on duty are always addressed as "sir" or "ma'am." We were a Navy family and both my parents made sure that was a rule I always followed.

"Well, then," she said, "I know this must all be a shock to you, but I'm thinking there must be a lot of questions you want to ask. We'll try to answer them for you if we can."

"Just one," I said, struggling to keep my voice under control. "How do you know they aren't dead? How do you know they weren't killed the minute they hit the ground?"

"We don't know that Connor," she sighed. "At this point we don't know anything for a fact except that your father's plane was lost. I wish— Captain Reynolds and I both wish—we had something more conclusive we could tell you. For now, all we can do is hope for the best and wait until we get more information."

The four of us sat in silence for a few minutes. Lieutenant Commander Salazar asked whether we would like her to offer a prayer. Mom said no, thank you, maybe another time. Then, when no more questions were forthcoming, Captain Reynolds stood up to leave. Lieutenant Commander Salazar followed.

"Doctor Ward, Connor, one of our support teams will be in touch with you tomorrow. They'll go over other information and make sure you get whatever assistance you need until this is resolved. For now, let me just say that all the way up the chain of command, the United States Navy is one-hundred percent behind you, and that we are sorry to have to bring you this unhappy news."

They both saluted my mother and me. And then they were gone, leaving us alone in a house that now seemed empty and lifeless.

CHAPTER THREE

Mom and I sat quietly for a few moments, each of us lost in our own thoughts, trying to make sense out of what we had just heard.

"Mom," I said, but she seemed to be a million miles away.

She turned her head toward the kitchen. "I should go and clean up the mess I made in there. There's glass all over the floor. I expect neighbors will begin showing up at the door before long, and I can't have the kitchen looking this way. You know how word gets around when something like this happens."

"Mom," I said again, "please. Forget the glass for a minute. I'll take care of it."

She turned to look at me, and I could see her face was empty of all expression.

I said, "What if he's dead? What if his 'chute didn't deploy, or what if the enemy found him as soon as he hit the ground?" I could feel the back of my neck getting hotter and tears forming in my eyes. "What if he landed in a tree and they shot him before he even had a chance to cut himself loose?"

Mom came over and sat down next to me. She pulled me close and hugged me for a long moment. Then she said, "It's going to be all right. You'll see. Search and rescue will probably retrieve Dad and Ensign Taney tomorrow. He'll be back aboard the *Constellation* before you know it. Then after the medics check him out, we'll fly over to the Philippines and have a reunion."

Her words were brave, but the uncertainty in her voice told a different story, as though this was a speech she had been practicing for a long time, hoping she'd never have to use it.

An hour later, just as Mom had predicted, the doorbell rang. Neighbors, both civilian and military, who had heard what happened were coming so see how we were doing and to bring food and express their sympathies.

Before I opened the door to the first of them, Mom said, "I know this is scary right now, Connor, and I know exactly what you're feeling inside. I feel it, too. And if you want to let it out, it's okay to do that. But don't do it in front of other people. We're Navy, Connor. Remember that. We don't cry or go all to pieces in public. We do our duty and keep our feelings inside, okay?"

"Okay," I said, and went to the door to greet the neighbors. But I didn't just want to cry. I wanted to scream.

****

Later that night, after the neighbors and friends had all finally gone home, Mom said, "Connor, do you think you'll be okay by yourself for a while? I need to run back by the hospital for a few minutes and check on a couple of patients I've been keeping an eye on."

"Sure," I said, "Go ahead. I'll be fine." I knew there were no patients she needed to see. She just needed to be doing something to take her mind off the night's events.

She was gone for about an hour, getting home just before midnight. I was awake in bed when she came in but decided not to bother her. After a while, I heard her in her bedroom, crying. I knew better than to ask her how she was, because it was important to her to keep a brave face. Like Dad, she was Navy, through and through.

Besides, I had stuff of my own to think about. Like how, if things didn't turn out for my dad, if he didn't survive the crash, or if he was killed by the enemy without being given a chance to surrender, what I was going to do to even the score?

CHAPTER FOUR

Three days went by, then a week, then ten days, with no further word about Dad and Ensign Taney. The day after Captain Reynolds and Lieutenant Salazar informed Mom and me that Dad's plane had been lost, we were contacted by a support team made up of two Navy and two Marine officers. Mostly they talked to Mom about financial stuff, like how we would continue to receive Dad's paychecks, since, until he was formally declared killed in action, or KIA, he was considered to be on active duty. They talked about insurance and counseling services, if we needed it. And although they were kind and sympathetic, after they left, Mom and I were still stuck with the realization that, at best, Dad was MIA, and nothing anyone could say to us was going to change that.

As the days passed, Mom seemed to be busier than ever at the hospital. Wounded Marines, since they were the ones seeing a lot of the combat action in Vietnam, made up a steady flow of new admissions. A lot of nights Mom either got home late, or else came home for supper and then went back to work for a few hours. I wasn't completely sure, but if I had to guess, I would have said she'd rather be working than sitting around the house waiting for another notification detail to arrive at the door with news that would break both our hearts.

Things weren't a whole lot better for me. With the baseball season over, there was nothing left to do after school except come home to an empty house. Sometimes Bobby Sachs would come over, but he had a lawn-mowing job that kept him busy, so a lot of the time I was by myself. Mornings, Mom would drop me off, and in the afternoon, I'd take the bus or catch a ride with one of the other kids' moms. Things seemed different at school, too. It was as if I had suddenly caught some dread disease that made other kids, including those I thought were my friends, avoid me in the lunchroom and between classes. A lot of them, I knew, had parents in the Navy or the Marines, and hanging around me probably made them worry that my family's bad luck might somehow be contagious.

My teachers weren't much better. The first day or two, I got a lot of "let me know if there's anything I can do to help," or "we're all praying for you and your Mom." But then that stopped, too. And although nobody ever said anything right out, I got the definite feeling the teachers were all taking it easy on me in class, like maybe my IQ had dropped by fifty points since Dad went missing. Not that it really mattered much, anyway. The school year was almost over and both teachers and kids seemed to be just marking off the days until we could all go home for the summer.

At first, I thought maybe I had done or said something wrong to somebody and said so to Bobby Sachs during lunch break.

"It's not that," he said. "It's just that nobody knows what to say to you, Connor. Don't take this wrong, but it's like when somebody in the family dies and then people come to the funeral and say stupid shit like, 'He's in a better place.' He might or might not be, or he might not be anyplace at all. But it doesn't make you feel better and they know it. But they can't think of anything else, so after a day or two the easiest thing is to just not say anything at all."

"I get that," I told him, "but I'm the same person I was last week. Everybody ought to know that by now."

"Well, that's just it. They don't know you that well. When did you come here, beginning of this year?"

I nodded my head and poked disinterestedly at a soggy French fry on my plate.

"Where were you before that?"

"We were in Pensacola, Florida."

"And how about before that?"

"Great Lakes Naval Air Station in Lake Forest, Illinois. And before that, Albany, Georgia."

Bobby said, "Do we need to keep going? Look, Connor, I'm your friend. I don't know why, 'cause sometimes you can be really weird—and here, I knew he was trying to make me laugh—but I am, and I probably always will be, even if you move another hundred times.

"But except for the guys on the team, nobody else has had much of a chance to get to know you that well. Plus, we all know that guys like you . . .."

"You mean Navy brats," I finished for him.

"Yeah, okay, Navy brats, call it that. Everybody knows you might not be sticking around for long, so, you know."

"Yeah, I know," I said, and wondered if things could get any worse.

CHAPTER FIVE

It did not take long for me to find out that things not only could get worse, they did. And they did it quickly.

On the Friday before school ended for the summer, Mom came home early from the hospital. Only instead of making supper like she usually did, she suggested that we go out to eat, and she offered to let me pick where we should go. If it had just been me, I would have said McDonald's, or maybe In-and-Out, but I was pretty sure neither one of those would have been Mom's first choice, so I suggested a Chinese restaurant near the mall. Mom said that was fine, so that was where we ended up. Besides, I could tell from the nervous way she was acting there was something she wanted to talk to me about, and I didn't think a noisy fast-food restaurant would be the right place.

After we were seated and had placed our order, the waitress brought us a pot of tea and two cups. When the waitress left to take our order to the kitchen, Mom said, "There's something I need to tell you."

"Is it about Dad? Did you hear something?"

She took a sip of her tea. "I did, but it's not about Dad, it's about me. And you."

"What about me?"

"I've received a summons to active duty. The situation in Vietnam has gotten worse since Tet, and the Marines need doctors at our hospital in Tokyo. You already know the Marines don't have a medical corps, so they rely on Navy doctors and nurses. It's a short-term assignment, just for ninety days. June, July and August."

I could feel the room start to spin around. *How could this be happening? What the hell is the matter with the Navy? First, I lose Dad and now they're asking my mother to ship out?*

I said, "When?"

"I have orders to be in San Francisco on the twenty-eighth. My deployment runs from the beginning of June through the end of August. Unless something changes, I'll be back before school starts again in the fall."

I started to say something, but Mom put her hand on my arm. That was the signal for "don't talk, just listen."

Mom said, "Connor, I don't like this any better than you do. Shipping out was certainly not my choice and I didn't volunteer, if that's what you're thinking. But if they had given me a choice, I still would have gone. I have a duty, just as your father does, and if I can help save some lives, I'm not going to refuse."

"So, what then? Am I supposed to go to

Tokyo with you?"

"That might be a good learning experience, but since you don't speak any Japanese, and I'll be bunking at the hospital, the answer is no. You're going to be spending the summer with your grandfather. Before I head out for San Francisco, we'll put you on the train here in Fresno. Your grandfather will meet you in Wichita. He knows you're coming and he's looking forward to having you. Plus, when I talked to him, he said there was a traveling league baseball team you could try out for. At least that will give you something to do while you're there."

"Great, I said. "Does it matter that I have zero interest in spending three months with him in Kansas?"

"Be sure and tell him that when you get there. I know he'll appreciate hearing you say so." She paused while the waitress brought our food and placed it on the table, making a show of lifting the lids off the various covered dishes.

"Look," she said, after the waitress had gone, "if it makes you feel better, think of it this way. Suppose your father were injured and hospitalized and some doctor who might be able to help him said, 'Sorry, I can't be bothered. I've got things to do here at home.'"

Noting like an extra helping of guilt. She

had me, and we both knew it, but I wasn't quite ready to give up.

"I get it. I really do. It's just that . . . it's just—Mom, isn't there ever going to be a time where we can stay in one place long enough to settle in, and make some real friends? It seems like no sooner do we begin to meet people than it's time to say goodbye all over again. Is this ever going to stop? I mean, if somebody asks me where I'm from, I don't even know what to say."

"I know," she said. "And for what it's worth, maybe this will help. Both your father and I have spent our entire adult lives in the Navy, and before his last deployment we talked about resigning our commissions and finding someplace to settle down, maybe here in California, maybe somewhere else. We're as tired as you are of all this moving around. I can easily catch on with a hospital or go into a private practice, almost anywhere."

"You'd really do that?" This was news to me, and the only question I could think of was, "What about Dad? What can he do?"

"He's a pilot. He can fly for an airline. Plus, he has a degree in aeronautical engineering. He can work for North American or Grumman or one of the other aircraft manufacturers. He'll probably find a job before I do. We just have to be patient for another year or so. You think you can hang on that long?"

Neither one of us had much to say on the ride back from the restaurant. Mom, I knew, had a million things she had to get done before she shipped out for Japan in a little more than a week. For my part, I was thinking about what it would be like to start and finish high school in one place and have a chance to make friends and then hold on to them for more than just a year or two. And then my thoughts drifted back to the prospect of spending the entire summer in a small town I'd never heard of with a grandfather I'd seen so seldom I didn't know whether I would even recognize him.

And to be completely honest, even though I wanted to be mad at the United States Navy, I really couldn't. Mom was right. We were a military family, and that meant that, for a little while longer at least, we had to do things we didn't always want to do.

So instead, I thought about the promise I had made to myself to find some way to get even for what I was sure had happened to Dad. And I wondered how I was going to be able to do that when I would be stuck in the middle of Kansas.

CHAPTER SIX

The next few days came and went so quickly it was like they were on wheels. First there was the end of the school year, followed by a graduation party where we all got handed yearbooks. With nearly two hundred kids in my ninth-grade class, most of the time at the party was spend signing the yearbooks, making promises to get together during the summer, and hope-to-see-you wishes for the next year when we would all be back together in high school.

At the end of April, counselors from Central Valley had visited the ninth-grade homerooms handing out lists of classes we would be required to take as well as a much shorter list of elective classes that were available. The high school athletic director talked about the various sports we could go out for providing we had no failing grades, and the assistant principal got everybody together in the gym to explain the high school's dress code and disciplinary policy. I knew there were other kids in my class who came from Navy and Marine families, and I wondered if they were thinking the same thing as me, which was, "am I even going to be here next year, or will we be posted someplace else?"

Finally, there was the graduation assembly and then the dance. At the graduation, all the kids were called up in alphabetical order and got handed an empty folder that would hold their diplomas when they got mailed out a couple weeks later. They did it this way so that if anybody bombed their finals, or didn't show up, or got out of order when the names were called, the actual diplomas wouldn't get mixed up as they were handed out.

And then there was the dance. I didn't particularly want to go, but I knew it might be my last chance to see some of my friends until school started in the fall. And since I didn't have a regular girlfriend, I ended up going with some of the guys from the baseball team. It wasn't a formal dance, like a prom. Nobody showed up in a rented tux, and the girls didn't wear formals or corsages, but the guys did wear coats and ties and the girls wore summer dresses and high-heeled shoes.

For most of the time, I sat in the gym bleachers with the guys I played sports with, drinking Cokes and talking about what we were planning to do over the summer. Some of the guys were looking forward to camping, or rafting, or just hanging out at the park district swimming pool. Others complained about having to go on vacation with their families to Disneyland or Yosemite Park or other boring places where families usually visited. Since I was going to be spending my summer in a town in Kansas nobody had ever heard of, I just sat and listened, and thought how great it would be if only my dad was home and we could do something together, no matter how boring it might seem to other people.

Finally, it was close to eleven o'clock, and the disc jockey announced the next two songs would be the final ones for the night, adding that "if you want to have a couple of slow dances with your special someone, this is your last chance."

To my surprise, when a song called "Moon River" came on, a girl named Laura Westcott walked over and asked me if I'd like to dance with her. I pretty much suck when it comes to dancing, so I started to say no thanks, and then decided, why not? I knew Laura from a couple of my classes and we would sometimes talk at lunch, or during passing periods. She was tall and slender and pretty and a very good softball player. And since the girls' and boys' teams always played on the same days, I sometimes visited with her between games or on the team bus coming back from an away game.

"I was sorry to hear about your dad, Connor," she told me after the music started. "Have you heard anything more since . . . well, since, you know." She let the question trail off without finishing it.

"It's okay," I said. "And no, we still don't know what happened after his plane went down.

We're hoping he found a place to hide out in the jungle or with friendlies until a rescue team can find him."

"It's a terrible war," she said. "My cousin was in the Army. He lost one of his legs when he stepped on a Bouncing Betty. Do you know what that is?"

I did. A Bouncing Betty is a small, anti-personnel mine that gets popped out of the ground by a spring when someone steps on it, exploding when it gets a couple of feet into the air, scattering metal fragments in all directions.

"He was in the hospital for three months. He got torn up pretty badly. I just hope this war gets over soon."

"I know," I said. "We all do."

"Moon River" ended and the last song of the night, "Never My Love" began to play.

"What are your plans for the summer, Connor?" Laura asked. "Are you doing anything special, or just staying close to home?"

"Neither one," I said. I explained that my mother was a doctor and that she had been assigned to a military hospital in Japan for three months and that I would be spending the summer with my grandfather in Kansas.

"Then you won't be around at all?"

"No. I'm leaving on the train the day after

tomorrow. I'm not even finished packing yet."

"I'm sorry," Laura told me. "I was hoping—listen, if I give you my address, will you write and let me know where you are? That way, I can write back and tell you what's going on around here. That is, I will if that's something you'd like me to do."

"What? Yeah, sure, absolutely," I said, enlightenment coming to me like a flashbulb in a dark closet. "I'd like that a lot."

When the music ended, Laura said, "Wait here," and ran off to get something out of her purse. When she came back, she had a slip of paper in her hand. As she passed it to me, she kissed me briefly on the cheek and said, "Write soon. I'll see you when you get back." And then she was gone.

Later that night, when I was in bed, I had a hard time getting to sleep. Maybe I was still worrying about Dad, or maybe it was the knowledge that I only had one more night at home before it was time to head east. Or maybe I was excited by the promise of what had happened earlier in the evening. But whatever it was, sleep did not come easily.

CHAPTER SEVEN

At eight o'clock in the evening on Sunday, May 26, Mom and I were at the Santa Fe Railway station in Fresno, waiting for the arrival of the *San Francisco Chief*, a train that ran between Richmond, across the bay from San Francisco, and Chicago, 2,500 miles and 50 hours east. I was only ticketed as far as Wichita, Kansas, two nights and one day away. My grandfather would be meeting the train at Wichita, and from there we would be driving another hour or so south to a town called Goldenrod, where my grandparents settled after World War II.

The train got into Fresno about ten minutes late. There was a pretty big crowd waiting to board the coach cars in the front of the train, but instead of waiting with the other people, Mom and I walked toward the back of the train where only a few people had gathered. I had left my sea bag with the baggage man inside the depot and carried only a small suitcase that held enough clean clothes, plus toiletries, for the time I would be on the train.

"I got you space in a sleeping car," Mom said. "You'll have a roomette to yourself, with a bed, so you won't be sitting up all night in a coach." I didn't know what she was talking about, although a bed sounded better than a coach seat. In fact, I didn't know anything at all about trains except that they sometimes stopped traffic at crossings and that, if you put a penny on the tracks, the train would mash it flat when the wheels rolled over it.

I asked Mom why I couldn't just fly to Wichita rather than spending thirty-two hours on a train.

"If you flew," she told me, "you'd have to take a connecting flight from Fresno to Los Angeles, then to Denver and then to Wichita. Besides, you've never traveled by train. You'll get to see some of the country instead of just flying over it."

I wasn't convinced, and it must have showed, because she added, "You'll see. It'll be fun."

A porter wearing a white jacket greeted us as we approached my assigned car. He checked my ticket and said, "Yes, sir, you're in number five. Soon as we get moving, I'll come by and see what time you'd like your bed turned down." Then he took my suitcase and placed it in the vestibule of the car. "No need to bother with that," he said. "I'll bring it to your room first thing."

Wait, I really had a room? To myself?

"Well," Mom said, "I guess this is so long for a while. I'll give you a phone call just as soon as I get to Tokyo. Meantime, give my love to your grandfather and tell him I said thanks."

"You mean for putting up with me all summer?"

"Sounds about right," she said. "Try not to give him a hard time. He didn't deal this mess."

Neither did I, I wanted to shout, loud enough to be heard all the way back to Kansas.

But then, Mom didn't, either. So instead, I said, "I understand."

Up front, at the other end of the train, there were two short blasts of the locomotive's air horn. A conductor called, "Bo-o-oard!" and doors began banging shut up and down the length of the train. Mom said, "Give me a hug," and then she said, "I love you. I'll miss you every minute."

"Me, too," I said.

And then the train began to move, and I was leaving home, on my way to Kansas.

CHAPTER EIGHT

By the time the train got to Bakersfield, I had walked from one end of the train to the other. Not counting the baggage and mail cars at the front of the train, I went through four coaches, all of which were crowded enough that I was glad I wasn't stuck there for a day-and-a-half; a lounge car, which I discovered had a upper level that was basically a glass dome that ran the length of the car—I stayed there long enough to drink a Coke and eat a bag of chips; a dining car that had already shut down for the night; and five sleeping cars. By the time I got back to my own small bedroom, I found the porter had somehow turned the seat I had been sitting in earlier into a bed and had stowed my overnight bag on an overhead rack. Feeling worn out from the day, and having nothing else to do, I crawled under the covers, but left the window shade up so I could take in what little there was to see in the darkness outside. At first, I had a hard time falling asleep, since the bed was rocking and rolling with the movement of the train, but somewhere in the middle of the California desert I drifted off.

It was bright daylight outside when the porter knocked on the door to my room. I sat up in bed and pulled back the curtain that hung over the door.

"Morning, sir," he said. "The dining car is open for breakfast. If you care to get something to eat, I'll have your room made up by the time you get back."

When I walked into the dining car, I was surprised that I couldn't just sit down anywhere I wanted. Instead, the steward, as he was called, seated me at a table with two uniformed Army officers, one a captain, whose name tag read "Berman." The other officer was a first lieutenant named Wilkinson. It was common practice in railroad dining cars, I learned, to seat customers as they came into the car at any available seat, regardless of who else might be sitting at that table.

Rather than give my order verbally to the waiter, I wrote it down on a special slip of paper—something else I found out that railroads do that nobody else does—and handed it to the waiter. One of the officers, Lieutenant Wilkinson, sitting across from me said, "Hey, kid, where you heading? Is it summer vacation already?"

"It is," I said, "but that's not where I'm going. My mom is sending me to spend the summer with my grandfather in Goldenrod, Kansas."

"Never heard of it," he said. "Where is it?"

"South of Wichita," I told him. "That's where I'm getting off."

"Okay," Captain Berman said, "so where's

home?"

"We live in Fresno. I got on the train last night."

"And your mom doesn't want you hanging around the house all summer? You didn't get in some kind of trouble, did you? Maybe forgot to get a haircut?"

He was referring to the fact that I had let my hair grow so that it hung partway over my ears and touched my shirt collar in the back. By contrast, the two officers seated across from me, like all military personnel, had their hair cut "high and tight," as required by regulations.

"No, sir. My mom is a Navy doctor. She's been assigned to a military hospital in Japan until the end of August."

"So then, is your dad in the Navy too?"

I nodded. "He's a pilot. He flies an F4. He got shot down near the DMZ a couple weeks ago. So far that's all we know. He's MIA."

That seemed to take all the kidding out of the two officers. They looked at each other for a moment, and then the captain spoke up.

"What's your name, son?"

"Connor Ward, sir. My father is Lieutenant Commander Richard Ward, USN. My mother is Lieutenant Commander Madeline Ward, MD, USN.

"Well, Mister Ward," the captain said, "The

Lieutenant and I would consider it a privilege if you'd allow us to buy your breakfast."

"Oh. Thank you, sir, but you don't need to do that. I have money from home."

Captain Berman sat up straight in his chair. "Mister Ward, are you telling me you're going to refuse a request from an officer in the United States Army to allow him to buy you a meal?" His voice sounded stern, like he was issuing an order, but there was a smile on his face.

"No, sir," I said, in what I hoped sounded like a military voice, "I am not. And thank you both."

As they finished their coffee and got up to leave, Lieutenant Wilkinson said, "Good luck to you, Mister Ward. And don't give your mother anything else to worry about. She's got plenty on her plate as it is."

I had to agree with that.

After I finished my breakfast, I walked up ahead and found a seat in the dome section of the lounge car. I spent most of the rest of the day drinking Cokes and watching out the windows as the train rolled through the Arizona and New Mexico deserts, and towns like Flagstaff, Winslow, Albuquerque, Belen and Clovis. By the time we got to Vaughn, New Mexico, I was hungry and tired of scenery, so I wandered back to the dining car and ordered a hamburger and a piece of cherry pie. Then, with darkness gathering, I went back to my bedroom for my last night on the train.

About nine-thirty, the porter came by my bedroom and asked if I wanted the bed made down. I went out into the corridor and watched as he went about his work. When he finished, he told me that we were now running on time and that we would be arriving in Wichita, on schedule, at seven o'clock in the morning.

"Diner's open at six," he said. "Do you want me to wake you in time for breakfast in the morning, or do you want to sleep a little longer and have your mornin' meal when you get off?"

"My grandfather is meeting me in Wichita," I told him. "I'll wait and see what he wants to do." We agreed that six-fifteen would be a good time for a wake-up call.

As the train rolled east through the Texas panhandle, I laid in bed and thought about my grandfather, whom I had not seen in at least five years.

Because we moved around a lot due to Mom and Dad's Navy careers, we only had a chance to visit with family on rare occasions. The last time had been for my grandmother's funeral, when Mom and I went to Kansas for the service. Like Mom and

Dad, my grandfather also served in the military, during World War II. Because of his imperfect eyesight he did not see combat, however, but stayed stateside as a company clerk at Fort Sam Houston, in Texas. After the war he mustered out, and with the help of the G.I. Bill, enrolled at Washburn University in Topeka, Kansas. He earned a law degree, went home to Goldenrod to become a small-town lawyer, then a justice of the peace and finally a county judge. My grandmother, meanwhile, first became a teacher and then stayed home to raise my mother and her two brothers. One of Mom's brothers, my Uncle Paul, was killed in a car accident before I was born. My other uncle, Jonathan, went to work for an oil company and has lived most of his life overseas.

After Mom and Uncle Jonathan were grown up and married, Grandmother went back to teaching. A few years after that, she had a heart attack and died at the age of fifty-seven. Since then, my grandfather has lived by himself in the house he and my grandmother built when they were first married.

As promised, the porter rapped on the door to my bedroom at quarter after six. I put on my jeans and a short-sleeved shirt and waited while he turned my bed back into a seat. After he finished, I ran water in the sink to wash up the best I could in the small space available in my room. Not long after, the train was backing into the station at Wichita. The porter placed my suitcase on the platform and told me that my sea bag would be available at the baggage room inside the station in about ten minutes.

CHAPTER NINE

By the time I found my way to the baggage room, my sea bag was there waiting. So was my grandfather. And despite my earlier worries, I recognized him right away. He was older, but still tall and clean-shaven with short gray hair and gold, wire-rimmed glasses. He was wearing a dark blue suit, a white shirt and a red and blue striped tie. His black shoes were polished to a high gloss. He looked so stern and proper standing there that if I didn't already know who he was, I might have mistaken him for the president of the Santa Fe Railway.

"Hello, Connor," he said when he spotted me. "It's been a while. How was your trip?"

"Okay, I guess. Long. I never traveled on a train before."

"Evidently, they didn't have a barber shop on the train," he said, another reference to the length of my hair. My first thought was that he might make me get a haircut to match his own, but then he smiled and gave me an awkward handshake.

"Come on, grab your gear. We've got to be in court by ten." I must have given him a funny look, because he added, "Well, you don't have to be there, at least not yet, but I do. I got to hand down a little country justice."

"Are you going to throw somebody in jail, Grandpa?"

"I don't think so. Not today, anyway. But maybe we'll be able to slow him down for a little while."

"Slow him down?"

He nodded. "Youngster name of Robbie Curtis. Today'll do him some good. Come on, I'll tell you about it on the way down to Goldenrod."

Grandpa had parked his car, a big blue Cadillac, right in front of the station, in a ten-minute parking zone. A policeman was standing next to car with a ticket book in his hand. While I stowed my sea bag in the trunk, Grandpa went over and said something to the policeman, who touched his hand to the bill of his cap, then shook Grandpa's hand and walked away.

"How come he didn't give you a ticket?" I asked.

"Professional courtesy," Grandpa said, as we drove away from the station. "You have anything to eat on the train?"

"No, but it's okay. It's still too early in the morning for me to be hungry. I can wait until lunchtime."

On the drive south toward Goldenrod, Grandpa explained that his court date had to do with a speeding ticket.

"Ordinarily, I don't get involved with traffic offenses. We got a JP who does that, but this one's a little bit special. You'll see when we get there." After that, he had questions about Dad, and whether we had found out anything more since the original visit from the notification detail.

"Not yet, but we're not giving up. As far as the Navy is concerned, he's missing in action. We're hoping that somehow he and Ensign Taney, that's his flight officer, managed to escape into the countryside and are making their way toward friendly territory."

"Is that what your mom thinks?"

"It's more like what she's praying for."

"And what are you praying for, Connor?"

I said without hesitation, "That this war will be over with, and no more families will answer their doorbell to find a notification detail on the front porch. The rest of the time, I just try not to think about it."

"Hold on to that prayer, Connor. It's a good one."

CHAPTER TEN

It took a little under an hour of driving through what seemed to be an endless expanse of wheat and cornfields to get from Wichita to Goldenrod. The Sunflower County courthouse in Goldenrod occupied the center of a town square that that also included a bank, a Sears department store, a drug store, a dress shop and a restaurant that advertised "Home Cooking." Most of the downtown structures were either one- or two-stories tall, except for the Eldridge Hotel, which had four. At about nine-thirty Grandpa wheeled into the parking lot behind the courthouse and parked in a space protected by a sign that read "Judge Evans."

"You've got your own parking space?" I was impressed.

"It wouldn't do for the judge to be late for court because he was driving around the square looking for a place to park, now would it?" I had to agree that it wouldn't, but from the small number of cars and trucks parked downtown, finding a space seemed as though it would be the least of his problems.

Grandpa and I entered the courthouse through the back door and rode the elevator up to the second floor. At the end of the hallway opposite the elevator was a heavy wooden door with a frosted glass window. A sign next to the door read "Judges Chambers—No Admittance."

"Come on," Grandpa said. "We have a few minutes before people start showing up. I'll give you a look at the courtroom."

We went through a doorway into the courtroom. It looked a lot like the ones I had seen on television. It was a large space with a wood railing that divided it approximately in half. Behind the railing, which held a swinging gate, were seats for spectators and trial witnesses who had already testified, if they wanted to stick around and watch the rest of the trial. In front of the railing were two tables, which I recognized as being for the prosecutor and the defense lawyers, a witness-stand and a jury box with fourteen chairs. Grandpa said that twelve of the chairs were for the actual jurors and the other two were for the alternates, people who would be asked to take over in the event one of the actual jurors couldn't be around to finish the trial for some reason.

Grandpa said, "Anybody gives me a song and dance about being too busy to serve, I make 'em alternates. That way they have to sit through the whole trial for nothing. Teaches a good lesson about civic duty."

The bench where the judge sat was reached by climbing a couple of stairs, so that the judge sat higher than everyone else and could see the entire courtroom from his seat. Overhead there were fluorescent lights and several ceiling fans which were turning lazily, stirring the already-warm air in the room.

"Why don't you just take a seat anywhere there behind the railing," Grandpa said. "I've got one or two things I need to do before we get started."

"Okay, Grandpa," I said, and found a spot where I could sit and wait.

After a few minutes the door to the hallway opened and a man wearing a suit that didn't seem to quite fit came in along with a boy who appeared to be about my age, or maybe a year older. The man looked tired, and maybe a little bit nervous, as if he wasn't used to being inside a courtroom and wasn't looking forward to the experience one bit. The boy was tall and stocky, with red hair and a splash of freckles across his cheeks. He had on blue jeans, a white shirt and a tie, and a sport coat that was several sizes too large and that probably came from his father's closet.

They both looked around the room, unsure what they were supposed to do, and then took seats across the aisle from where I was sitting. In another minute, a deputy sheriff entered the room and stood near the bench where my grandfather would be sitting. He was followed by a lady carrying a case that contained what looked like a typewriter. When she got settled, my grandfather entered through the door next to the bench and the deputy called out in a loud voice, "All rise. This court is now in session, the honorable Harold F. Evans presiding."

We all stood up and waited until my grandfather took his seat at the bench. "Thanks, everybody," he said. "Give me just a minute here and then we'll get started." He glanced briefly at some papers he had brought in with him, then motioned for the man and the boy who came in after me to approach the bench.

"Just for the record, for you both, what we're doing here is not a trial. We don't have a prosecutor or a jury, and we won't be calling any witnesses or the arresting officer. Instead, we're just going to have a short conversation, and if everybody's agreed when we get finished, we can all go home and get back to whatever we were doing. Does that sound okay?"

When nobody spoke up, Grandfather said, "Mr. Curtis, you and your boy will have to answer my questions verbally so we can get everything on the record. You can't just shake your heads because the reporter won't be able to record your answers, you understand?"

"Yes, Judge," said the man Grandfather

called Mr. Curtis.

"Robbie, do you understand?" The boy, Robbie Curtis, said, "Yes, sir."

"Okay, good, then let's see what we've got here. According to the report from the deputy who pinched you down, Robbie, you were stopped last week Wednesday at one o'clock in the morning for speeding out on the county road doing a hundred and fifteen miles an hour. I believe that road is posted for forty-five, so you were seventy miles an hour over the speed limit. That sound about right?"

So softly that I could barely hear, Robbie nodded and said, "Yes, sir."

Grandpa said, "You need to speak up, son, so the recorder can hear you."

"Yes, sir," Robbie Curtis said, this time in a louder voice.

"Okay, good. It also says you were driving a Chevy Corvette. You're stepping up in the world some. Is that your car, Robbie?"

Mr. Curtis spoke up. "The boy's got a part time job washing cars over to the dealership. He needs the keys to drive 'em through the car wash."

"I see," Grandfather said. "So, you just kind of took the long way around getting to the wash, is that it?"

When neither Robbie nor Mr. Curtis said anything, Grandfather went on. "Robbie, I've got your driver's license here, which the deputy took from you when he wrote you up. It says here your birthday is September ninth, when you'll be seventeen. Now I know that's a pretty frisky age, but you still can't be driving that fast on any roads in this county, even if it is at a time of night when you're not likely to see any other traffic. Wouldn't you agree?"

"Yes, sir, I guess so."

"I guess so, too," Grandpa said. "So, here's what we're going to do. I already know you're saving up your money for college and you need your job. I also talked to Don Robinson at the Chevy dealership and he says you're a good worker, and since you didn't wreck the car, he's willing to keep you on so long as you don't take any more joyrides.

"Meantime, I'm going to let you keep your license with the understanding that you can only drive to and from your job. That limitation will stay in place until school starts in the fall, and then you can have it back with no restrictions, provided you don't get caught driving outside of work hours between now and then. If that happens, you'll be a-walkin' until you're eighteen, understand?"

"Yes, sir."

"And?" Mr. Curtis said.

"Thank you, Judge," Robbie said.

"And?" Mr. Curtis said a second time.

"And I'm sorry. It won't happen again."

"Good," Grandpa said. "And I have one more thing, just to help you keep all this in mind. The court fines you one hundred dollars plus costs, which I will hold in abeyance as long as you stay out of trouble. If I see you back here before your birthday, you'll have to open up your wallet and hand over one hundred and twenty-five dollars, clear?"

"Yes, sir," Robbie said.

"Mister Curtis, you got anything you want to say?"

"Like the boy said, it won't happen again. I'll make sure of it."

"Okay, then." Grandpa banged his gavel on the bench and said, "We're adjourned. Mr. Curtis, if you and Robbie can stick around for just one more minute, I'd like to talk to you. Off the record, of course." Grandpa motioned for me to come forward.

Now what, I thought. I hadn't been in town long enough to do anything wrong, and I couldn't imagine what Grandpa had to say to me in court that he couldn't have said in the car on the way down from Wichita.

"Mr. Curtis, I understand you coach the boy's' baseball team here in Goldenrod. Do I have that right?"

"Yes, sir, that's right. We're doing pretty good, too. We won three in a row so far."

"Well," Grandpa said, motioning toward me, "this is my grandson, Connor. He's here from California. Going to spend the summer visiting with me. I expect he'll get around to telling you more about why when he's ready. Anyhow, scouting report from California says he's a pretty good ballplayer himself, and I'd appreciate it if you'd give him a tryout. I'm not saying you have to put him on the team. You're the coach, you make the call. Just give him a look-see and then you can decide if you want to keep him around."

Mr. Curtis nodded his head. "I guess that'd be all right. We can carry fifteen players. Right now, we're light one." He looked straight at Grandpa and I sensed that something unspoken passed between them.

Mister Curtis said to me, "We got a practice at the city park at six o'clock tonight. Come on by and we'll see how you do."

"He'll be there," Grandpa said.

And that was how I got a tryout with the Goldenrod Copperheads.

CHAPTER ELEVEN

After we left the courthouse, Grandpa and I stopped at the restaurant on the town square for lunch. I was surprised, after we were seated, at the number of people who came by our table to say hello to Grandpa, who in turn introduced me to all of them. He told me some of the people I met were local businessmen or farmers who had retained him when he still had his law practice, or who'd had business before his court. The rest were friends he and my grandmother had made over the lifetime they had lived in Goldenrod. One or two, I learned later, were even folks Grandpa had sent to jail for one reason or another. I quickly realized that in a town this size, everybody pretty much knew everybody else, and that when you were a judge, you were somebody special. Still, I wondered out loud about the people he had sent to jail.

"No hard feelings. They're just paying their respects," Grandpa told me. "It's kind of the way things work if you want to get along hereabouts."

"You mean if they're nice to you, you might do them a favor some day?"

"Like that Robbie Curtis you met a while ago? Do you think I did him a favor?"

"It seemed like it. I mean, you went pretty easy on him considering how fast he was driving."

Grandpa spread a pat of butter on a hunk of cornbread he picked out from the basket the waitress had placed on the table when we sat down.

"Robbie's a good kid, and his father is a decent man. Robbie needs his summer job. I figured between the two of them, they could use a break. Robbie didn't wreck the car or run over somebody's dog, and I don't believe his father has the money to pay for Robbie's college without help, so why not let this one slide a little bit? Of course," he added, "if he lays another egg like this last one, then we'll have to try some other way to get his attention."

The waitress brought our lunch order. Grandpa ordered a steak with mashed potatoes, green beans and black coffee. "Your usual, Judge," she said when she set the plate in front of him. "Just the way you like it." I had a hamburger and fries with a Coke.

I said, "Grandpa, what made you think Mr. Curtis would agree to let me try out for his baseball team? Was it because you gave him and Robbie a break?"

"I like to think a good team can always use another good player."

I wasn't so sure about that. "And why did you think I'd want to play for him?"

Grandpa took a sip of his coffee. "It's this way. I'm thinking you've had a pretty rough couple of weeks since you got the news about your dad. Now you're sitting here at the bottom end of Kansas where hardly anything ever happens and where it's so flat a person can watch his dog run away for three days. I just thought you might want something to do and maybe meet some people your own age. Otherwise, you'll be spending your time sitting on the front porch listening to the wind blow through the wheat fields. Of course, if that's what you'd rather do, it's okay with me."

"No, it's fine, I guess I'll give it a try."

Grandpa said, "Look, Connor, I know you're hurting right now, and I wish there was something I could do to make things better. But right now, I just don't know what that might be."

"I know. I understand. And Grandpa, I'm not upset because I'm here instead of back in California. If I knew Dad was okay, I'd be fine wherever I was. I'm a Navy brat. I'm used to moving around a lot. I don't like it, but Mom and Dad do what they do because they took an oath and because they think it's the right thing to do. It's just . . . I guess it's just the not knowing."

"Well, maybe we'll find out something soon. Your mom said she'd call as soon as she heard anything. Now come on, finish your lunch and I'll give you a two-minute tour of your new home for the rest of the summer."

"Two minutes? That's it?"

"Isn't very much to see. That's about all it's going to take."

Grandpa wasn't kidding about that. After we finished eating, he gave me the tour, and in fact, I'd already seen most of what there was to see. Apart from the businesses surrounding the courthouse square, Goldenrod was home to a hardware store, a place that sold sporting goods, the Chevrolet dealership where Robbie Curtis had "borrowed" the Corvette and a Dairy Queen drive-in. Goldenrod also had a Montgomery-Ward department store, a filling station, a Western Auto, a barber shop, a Ford dealer that also sold tractors and a lawyer's office. There were some other stores and businesses that ran for a block or so in each direction. The jail, I found out, was in the basement of the courthouse. Out on the highway leading out of town was a police and volunteer fire station, the county hospital, a feed store, a grain elevator, a motel, an A&P grocery store and a farm equipment dealer. A railroad track ran behind the grain elevator.

"Train comes into town couple times a week from Oklahoma to work cars at the grain elevator. That's about the most excitement we get around here, except, of course, for the Fourth of July picnic." He glanced over at me. "You even a little bit excited to be here?"

"Something like that," I told him, but inside I wondered how much longer it would be before my life finally hit rock-bottom.

CHAPTER TWELVE

"So," Grandpa said on the way home from our tour, "I guess we'll need to take a run by the sporting goods store and get you a glove and some spikes."

"I brought my stuff from home," I told him. "Mom said something about a traveling team, and I figured since I was going to be here all summer, I might find somebody to throw a ball around with."

When we got to Grandpa's house, which was a big, white-painted two-story with red shutters and a wide porch that wrapped around three sides, he showed me around and told me my bedroom would be upstairs. He said he preferred to sleep in the downstairs bedroom because, depending upon the weather, his knees sometimes hurt and he didn't want to have to use the stairs any more than necessary.

"I'm not going to be checkin' on it too much, but I expect you keep your bed made and your bathroom straightened up. Missus Mueller, you'll meet her tomorrow, she comes in every day during the week with her daughter Mary Alice to clean up a bit and fix supper. I gave her the day off today since I figured we'd be too busy to sit down for a meal." He looked at me like he still wasn't quite sure who I was or what I was doing in his house.

"I have a little bit of work to do back at the courthouse. You think you'll be okay here by yourself until I get back?"

"I'll be fine, Grandpa. Don't worry about me."

After he drove off, I went upstairs and got started unpacking my sea bag and arranging my clothes in the dresser and closet. I put my few toiletries in the bathroom. Then I laid down on the bed and tried to imagine how I was going to get through an entire summer in the middle of nowhere where I had no friends and nobody to talk to beside my grandfather who I hadn't seen more than five or six times in my entire life. Ten minutes later, I was asleep.

A little after five o'clock, I heard Grandpa calling from downstairs to ask if I wanted something to eat before it was time to go to baseball practice. I told him anything would be fine, but that I didn't want very much. I ended up eating a ham sandwich and drinking a glass of milk, and then it was time to go.

We got to the park a little before six. There were already four or five guys my age throwing a ball around, but since Grandpa said he wasn't sure what their names were, we took a seat on one of the benches and waited for Robbie and Mr. Curtis to show up. A few more players arrived, and then Robbie and Mr. Curtis drove up about ten after six. When they got out of Mr. Curtis's pickup, I noticed right away that Robbie had a dark purple bruise around his eye. Grandpa saw it, too, but he didn't say anything.

Mister Curtis removed a duffel bag full of bats from the back of his truck and handed it to Robbie. Then he walked over to where Grandpa and I were sitting.

"Ready to go?" he asked me.

"I guess so," I said. "What happened to Robbie's eye?"

He hesitated. "Robbie and me, we were, uh, we were throwin' a ball around in the back yard earlier today, and, well, I guess one got away. We put some ice on it right quick. He'll be okay."

"Glad to hear it," Grandpa said, but there was something in his voice that told me he didn't believe Mr. Curtis's explanation.

Mister Curtis told Robbie to take the bag with the bats and balls over to the first base dugout and empty it out.

"So, I didn't ask you earlier, Connor," Mr. Curtis said. "What position are you comfortable playing? Or do you play more than one?"

"I guess I'm what you'd call a mop-up man. In our JV league we have a rule that pitchers can only throw 90 pitches before they have to come out. When that happens, I generally go in and finish up. Once in a while, coach lets me play in the outfield, and sometimes I get sent in to pinch run for the slower guys."

"Well, we got pretty good outfielders as it is, but I guess it never hurts to have one more. Pitchers, though, we can sure use some help there, because we got the same 90-pitch rule. How about you and Robbie throw a few warmups and then let's see what you got. That is," he said, turning to Grandpa, "if it's okay with you, Judge."

"That's what we're here for," Grandpa said.

Robbie grabbed a catcher's mitt and threw me a ball. I walked out to the pitcher's mound while Robbie stood at home plate. We tossed a few soft ones back and forth to get loosened up and then Robbie squatted down behind the plate. "Okay, surfer boy, let's see what you got."

I said, "I live a hundred miles from the beach. And maybe you should put on a mask. I don't want to mess up your other eye."

"Just bring it. I'll catch it."

Mister Curtis walked over and stood behind the backstop where Robbie had set up. Grandpa came over from the bench and stood next to him, and the other players who had been throwing the ball around the outfield came in to check me out.

When I started seriously watching baseball on television, there were three great pitchers in the National League that I followed: Bob Gibson of the Cardinals, Juan Marichal of the Giants, both righthanders, and Sandy Koufax of the Dodgers, who, like me, was a lefthander. When I decided I wanted to be a pitcher, I studied each of them, watching them whenever I could on the "Game of the Week." And what I saw was that each of them had a very high leg kick which, I thought, must be the reason they all had a nearly unhittable fastball. And so, when I was just starting out, I tried to use the same leg kick, rocking back on the rubber and lifting my right leg as high as I could before pushing off and releasing the ball straight over the top. And what I learned was that, when I did that, I had absolutely no control over where the ball was going to end up. My first coach saw the same thing and got me to lower my leg kick and go to a three-quarter motion. Almost immediately I started throwing strikes with pretty good velocity.

"You gonna throw one or what?" hollered Robbie. And so, I wound up and uncorked a pitch that bounced three feet in front of the plate. The ball skipped off Robbie's mitt and rolled to left side of the backstop. Robbie retrieved the ball and threw it back to me.

"A little higher next time." I threw the next

one six feet over his head and watched it hit the screen right in front of where Grandpa and Mr. Curtis were standing. Grandpa just stared at me. Mr. Curtis shook his head slowly. Robbie started to say something and then saw me grinning.

"Showboat. You did that on purpose."

"Did I?" I asked with mock innocence. "Is this better?" And I fired a perfect strike right down the middle and just about knee-high if a batter was standing in the box. After that I threw ten more, low and away, low and inside, high and outside. I mixed in a couple of changeups, just because I could.

"Okay," said Mr. Curtis, "got it. Let's get a hitter in there." He pointed to one of the players standing along the foul line. "Dennis, grab a bat and a helmet and stand in the box. Let's give Connor something to throw at."

Dennis said, "You want me to swing, coach?"

"Take a couple and then swing away. Robbie, put your mask on. Couple of the rest of you, head on out to the outfield to shag whatever comes your way."

Robbie walked out to the mound and handed me the ball. "Connor, this here is Dennis Smith. He's our best hitter right now, somewhere north of .600. I don't think you'll get him out, but if he hits one back at you, just get out of the way so it don't take your head off."

"I got it," I said.

Dennis was a big kid with thick arms and legs and wide shoulders. He looked strong enough to yank the bumper off Grandpa's Cadillac and then bend it in half just to show that he still had something left in the tank.

Robbie walked back and took his position behind the plate. I threw a couple of pitches more or less down the middle to give Dennis Smith a look at my stuff.

"Ready?"

Dennis got into his stance. "Bring it."

I took a full windup and threw him a fastball over the outside corner. Dennis swung and missed. The next one was high and inside, but still in the strike zone. He swung and missed again, and I saw the other players who were watching us turn and look at one another. Three more pitches, two swings and misses and one foul tip.

"Okay, one more," Mr. Curtis called. "Connor, throw it down the middle this time. Let him hit it."

"Will do," I said, and served it up, waist-high, right down Broadway. Dennis gave a mighty swing and hit a weak popup that I only had to take about two steps toward shortstop to catch.

"Okay, come on in. Connor, shake hands

with Dennis Smith. He's our left fielder." We shook, but I could tell Dennis wasn't particularly happy to meet me.

"This here didn't mean anything," he said, scowling. "It wasn't a real game. And anyway, I never faced no left-hander in this league before."

"Then it was lucky for you this was just practice," I told him.

He didn't say anything to that. He just turned and walked back to the bench.

Mister Curtis introduced me to the rest of the team. It was a blur of names: Joe, Andy, David, Larry, Dan, Eddie, Craig, Junior, another David ("call me Dave"), Conrad and Johnny. Before the end of the season, which I found out was fourteen games, I was sure I'd know them all. But for the moment, except for Robbie, Dennis and the big first baseman named Junior, I'd already forgotten the rest.

Mister Curtis said that if I still wanted to play on the team, there were some papers I'd need to get filled out. He said since I was living with Grandpa, he could sign the consent form that would allow me to participate. The next game, I was told, was Saturday morning, here at the park, against a team from Caldwell, a town about ten miles away.

"First pitch is at ten-thirty," Mr. Curtis said. "Try to be here about an hour early for warmups and batting practice and I'll have a uniform for you. Only number we got left is fifteen. That okay with you?"

I said that was fine.

"Oh, and maybe put some ice on that elbow. We don't want you getting all swollen up."

Grandpa and I sat for a few more minutes and watched the rest of the team go through some more of their practice workouts, but we didn't stay long. Grandpa said he had some work to do, and I was dead tired from two days of train travel with very little sleep, so we said our good-byes and headed for home, but not before Grandpa stopped at the Dairy Queen and bought us each an ice cream cone.

I said, "Grandpa, what do you really think happened to Robbie's eye? I don't think he got hit with a ball unless his dad threw it when he wasn't looking. He's a better catcher than that. He caught everything I threw his way."

"I expect after they left the courthouse, Robbie and his dad got to talking seriously about that business with the Corvette." He shook his head slowly. "Some folks hereabouts have a few different ideas about how to teach their kids."

CHAPTER THIRTEEN

The next morning, I slept late, tired from the past two days' travel and my body clock still on California time. By the time I got dressed and showered and headed down to the kitchen, it was nearly eleven-thirty. I thought I'd be on my own for lunch, since I'd heard Grandpa drive away earlier, but when I got downstairs, I found two people, a woman who was about Mom's age working at the counter glazing a ham, and a pretty girl who looked to be about the same age as me with long brown hair and green eyes sitting at the table peeling potatoes and carrots.

"Good morning," the woman said when she heard me come into the kitchen. You must be Connor. The judge said you'd probably be coming down late this morning since you had a long day yesterday. My name is Loretta Mueller, but if you want, you can call me Loretta. And this," she said, gesturing toward the girl at the table, "is my daughter Mary Alice."

"Nice to meet you," I said into the space between them. "Have you been here all morning?"

"Lord, no," she said, laughing. "I come by every day right about this time to clean house and make supper for Judge Evans—I'm sorry, your grandfather. Mornings he just has coffee, and he has lunch downtown on days he's working, which is just about every day, so I don't usually get here until late morning. Now that school is out, Mary Alice is helping me out a little."

"Judge Evans says he expects you'll be here all summer," Mary Alice said. "He said your folks are in the Navy, is that right?"

I nodded. "My dad's a pilot. My mom is a doctor, and they both . . . they're both on active duty, so I needed a place to stay until they get back."

"I heard your dad might not be coming back. I heard he got shot down and nobody knows what happened to him."

"I guess that's right," I said.

Mrs. Mueller said, "Mary Alice!"

It wasn't like I had forgotten why I was in Kansas and not California, but I had been trying not to think about it. Hearing what Mary Alice just said reminded me all over again, and having it come from someone I had just met made me a little bit angry. Rather than say something I knew I would immediately regret, I went outside and took a seat on the back-porch steps. Inside, I heard Loretta say to Mary Alice, "What in the world is the matter with you? Get out there right now and tell him you're sorry."

After a few moments, Mary Alice came out

and sat down next to me. "I imagine you heard all that."

"Yeah, I did, but it's okay. Don't worry about it."

"No" she said, "I am sorry. It's just that sometimes I say the first damn thing that pops into my head. I don't mean to. It's just like there's a gate between my brain and my mouth that doesn't stay closed all the way and then something stupid gets out."

"Mary Alice, everything you said was true. You don't have to apologize for that."

She nodded. "Just the same, it must be tough, not knowing."

"Yeah, it is. Plus, now instead of being home with people I know, I'm here—wherever here is—and my grandfather is stuck with me getting in his way for the next three months."

"Well, if you're worried about that, I don't think he feels like he's stuck. Since he found out you were coming, all he's been talking about is how great it will be to have you here. It sounds like he doesn't get to see you very often."

"No, he doesn't. I was pretty small the last time we were here and I don't remember much about it. And he's never been to any of the places we've lived."

After that we sat quietly for a few moments,

looking out across Grandpa's back yard to the tree line that separated the road from the back fence. And even though it was only a few minutes past noon, the day was already very hot, with no breeze and the sun hammering down from the bluish-white sky overhead.

"Hey," Mary Alice said, brightening. "You want to go get some lunch? I'll drive."

"You have your license?"

"Sure, don't you?"

"I have a permit, but I won't be sixteen until August."

"Then I'm older than you. I turned sixteen in April. I got my license the day after my birthday, and I only waited the extra day because my birthday was on a Sunday. And another thing. Only old people like my mother and father and the judge call me Mary Alice. Everybody else calls me Mal, okay?"

"Okay."

She disappeared into the house for a minute and then reappeared with her purse and a set of keys. "Let's go."

Mal's mother's car was an old two-door Ford, a maroon '52 or a '53. When she first started it up, a big cloud of blue oil smoke belched out of the tail pipe, and when we got going down the road, the car rattled and clattered like it had a load of scrap metal in the trunk.

"I call it the Crapmobile. It'll never be a guy magnet, but for getting around town it's better than walking."

We drove into town and then headed out the highway a couple of miles to a drive-in restaurant called Ted 'n' Ed's. From the number of cars in the parking lot and the kids hanging around, I realized that this was a popular spot for high school kids. Mal backed the Crapmobile into an open spot and turned off the engine.

"The menu's right here," she said, pointing to a sign mounted on a pole that also held a speaker, like at a drive-in movie. When we were ready to order she pressed a button and the speaker crackled to life. I ordered, what else, a hamburger, fries and a Coke. Mal wanted a strawberry malt with extra whipped cream.

"Mom and I ate something before you came down," she said. "This is just to keep me going until suppertime."

"We have places like this back in Fresno," I said. "Some places the carhops bring out the trays on roller skates."

"They tried that here for a while, but the 'hops weren't too good on skates. They kept falling down and spilling the food. So now they just walk it out."

While we waited for our order to show up, Mal said, "So, Connor Ward, do you have a girlfriend back in California?"

"Not really," I said, remembering at that moment that I had promised to send Laura Westcott Grandpa's mailing address. "There's this girl, Laura. We had some classes together this year and I told her I'd write and let her know where I am, but it's not like it's serious or anything. Besides, when you're in a military family, you move around a lot."

"You mean like now?"

"No. This is different. Both my parents were called up to active duty. There was nobody back in California I could stay with for the entire summer."

I started to ask her a question I was wondering about when our order arrived. Mal rolled her window up a couple of inches and the carhop, a girl about Mal's age with her hair pulled back into a long ponytail, hung the tray on the glass.

"Hey there, Mal," she said, smiling. "You got a new boyfriend?"

"This is Connor. He's staying with Judge Evans for the summer. Connor, this is Louise Porter. We're in the same class together at school."

"Hi, Louise," I said.

"Hi, Connor," Louise said. "Say, he's kinda cute, Mal. Does Denny know you guys are out together?"

"No, and you don't need to be telling him anything, either. Connor only got here yesterday. I'm just giving him the tour."

"If you say so." Louise leaned in the open window and gave me a smile. "Connor, I'm having a party at my house this Saturday. It's kind of a kickoff to summer. Maybe I'll see you there?"

"I don't know," I said, feeling my face turning red. "I don't really know anybody here yet and I'm not much fun at parties."

"Then this'll be your opportunity to turn a fresh page. I'll expect you to be there. Mal, honk when you're done and I'll come get your tray."

After Louise left, I said to Mal, "Who's Denny? Is that your boyfriend?"

"Denny Smith," she told me. "We broke up right before school got out. If you go to the party, you'll probably meet him."

"Already did," I told her. "There was a baseball practice last night. I threw a few pitches, just as a tryout. After I got warmed up the coach told him to get in the box and swing away, you know, to show me what he could do. I struck him out twice and popped him up once on seven pitches."

There was a pause and then she said, "Oh, no, this isn't going to be good."

"He'll forget about it. If I decide to play, I'll

be on the team with him, not against him."

"I'm not talking about baseball," Mal said. "Denny just pulled into the parking lot. He's got Robbie Curtis with him and they saw us."

CHAPTER FOURTEEN

Denny's car was a two- or three-year old Mustang. It had big tires in the back and small ones in the front, and when he gunned the engine before backing into a parking spot, a noise that sounded like automatic weapons fire exploded from the tailpipes. I didn't know a whole lot about cars, but I could tell from the racket this one was making that whatever he had under the hood was not what the Mustang left the factory with.

Denny shut off the engine and then he and Robbie got out of the car and walked over to where Mal and I were parked.

"Hey, Mal," Denny said, "got yourself a new boyfriend? Some cute little surfer boy from way out in California, it looks like."

"Get lost," she told him. "We're just having lunch."

"And then what? You gonna drive out to the lake for a little make-out session? I know you're never happier than when you're in the back seat of some dude's car." He looked over at me and balled his fists. "Hey, surfer boy, are you gonna just sit there and let me talk to your new girlfriend like that, or are you gonna do something about it?"

Oh, crap, not already. I got out of the car and walked around to where he was standing. "If you fight as well as you swing the bat, I don't figure I've got anything to worry about." But before anything else happened, Robbie jumped in between us.

"Connor," Robbie said, "get back in the car. You too, Denny. Go."

For a moment, nobody moved. Then Denny shrugged, grinned and walked back toward his jacked-up Mustang. "The next time you see me," he called over his shoulder, "I'll be swinging at your head. And it won't be with a baseball bat."

"Try that and see what happens."

Robbie turned to me. "You need to be careful around him. He gets riled easy."

"You know what, the hell with this." I was angry now. "Tell your old man I'm not going to play any baseball. Better yet, I'll tell him. I got enough to think about right now without getting into a fight over a girl I just met an hour ago."

Robbie appeared to give that some thought.

"Listen, Connor, I don't know you at all, and you might be okay, but right now that don't much matter. But for a while at least, we're gonna have to act like we're best pals, 'cause the only reason I ain't in juvie right now is your grandfather cut me a break, and the only reason he did that is so my old man would put you on this baseball team.

"So-o-o-o," he said, drawing it out to make

his point, "you see, you're gonna have to play, and the fact is, what I saw? You're the best pitcher we've got even before you put on a uniform. Now you let me worry about Denny and you can just concentrate on showing up and throwin' strikes, you got it?"

"We'll see," I said, and got back into the car, slamming the door hard.

"How about that?" Mal said after Denny and Robbie were gone. "You haven't even been here two days and already you've made a reputation for yourself. That has to be a record."

"He's an idiot. I've met plenty of guys like that."

"And you don't think I'm worth fighting over?" She tried to sound hurt, but her smile said she was teasing.

"I don't think it's you he wants to fight over. I made him look bad yesterday, and he's pissed off about it. He thinks if he beats me up it'll prove that he's better at something than I am and everybody will know about it."

"You're probably right, but you didn't answer my question."

"I got out of the car, didn't I? Isn't that enough?"

"You're sweet, Connor," she said, smiling. "Maybe before you go back to California, I'll end up fighting over you."

Driving back to Grandpa's house, Mal said, "You know, you're lucky Robbie stepped between you and Denny before something bad happened. Denny can get pretty crazy when he gets jacked up about something. He likes hitting people. I can tell you that for a fact."

"You used to go with him. Did he hit you?"

She nodded but kept her eyes on the road. "Twice. Once at a dance, because another boy asked me to dance. Denny thought I let him get a little too close, we got into an argument about it and he slapped me. It wasn't very hard, and I thought, well, maybe I had that coming. Plus, he acted all sorry and whatever, so I forgave him."

"What about the other time?"

"I don't want to talk about that."

"Okay," I said.

She drove another mile or so and then pulled off on the side of the road. She turned to face me, and I saw tears in her eyes.

"It was like this. We were at a party at Sandy Martin's house about a month before school let out. Denny and some of the other guys on the baseball team brought some beer. Pretty soon they all started getting loud and I heard Denny tell the other guys what he was going to do with me on the way home. I said I didn't like him talking about me like that. I said I wasn't some whore and I wasn't going to put up with him talking about me like that.

"He said I was his girl and he could talk about me whatever way he wanted. I told him I'd find another way home, and when I started to walk away, he grabbed me by the arm. He hit me and knocked me down. All the other kids saw him do it. I told him right then we were done, and I meant it.

"He tried calling me a few times after that, but I wouldn't talk to him. After a while he gave up. That's where we are now."

"I'm sorry," I told her, "that shouldn't have happened." And I wondered how tough he would feel if I put my best fastball into his ear.

CHAPTER FIFTEEN

"Well," Grandpa said over a delicious dinner of baked ham, mashed potatoes and green beans prepared by Mrs. Mueller, "I hear tell you and Mary Alice took a ride this afternoon." I didn't want to talk with food in my mouth, so I nodded, yes. "Where'd you get off to, or shouldn't I ask?"

Grandpa hadn't changed out of his dark suit and tie when he got home from the courthouse. To all appearances, he could have been discussing legal business with a group of lawyers instead of a fifteen-year-old kid wearing jeans and a t-shirt. He didn't say anything about how I was dressed, or my hair, for that matter, but I got the feeling he had expected I might dress a little better for our evening meal. Tomorrow night, I'd find something better to wear.

I swallowed and took a drink of my iced tea so I could talk. "We drove the Crapmobile— that's what Mal calls her mother's old Ford—to Ted 'n' Ed's. We had lunch and then came back. Mal said she had to help her mom get our supper ready."

"Well, they did a good job, don't you think?"

"I do," I said. "Do Mal and Mrs. Mueller ever stay and have supper with us—with you?"

"Once in a while is about all. Tom Mueller,

that's Loretta's husband. Tom's a veterinarian and sometimes he has to travel overnight to take care of some farmer's cow that's taken sick, or to deliver a calf or whatnot. When that happens, the ladies stay for supper. Other times, like tonight, they just take part of what they cooked home. I'm happy to let them have it. Otherwise, we'd be eating this ham for a week."

We finished our supper without talking about anything important. While we were clearing the table, I said, "Grandpa, can I ask you something?"

"You already did," he said, smiling at his little joke. "Or was there something else you were wanting?"

"Yes. When Mal and I were having lunch, we ran into Robbie Curtis and Dennis Smith. I know you know Robbie, but do you know Dennis at all?"

"That's that overgrown kid last night couldn't hit you with a boat paddle, isn't it?"

I nodded. "He's got a bad swing. He tries to turn every pitch he sees into a home run. Unless he gets past that, he'll never be able to hit good pitching. Anyhow, turns out Dennis and Mal—Mary Alice—used to go together, and she told me when they broke up it didn't go so well. I thought for a minute when Dennis saw us together there was going to be trouble. He said some things he shouldn't have, and Mal got pretty upset. Then he wanted to fight me because I was sitting in the car with her."

"Well, Dennis is a big kid. If you're wanting to fight him, better pack a lunch."

"Not my question, Grandpa."

"So then, what is it you're wanting to know?"

"Before we left Ted 'n' Ed's, Robbie told me the only reason you didn't send him to juvie for stealing that car is because his father agreed to let me try out for the baseball team. Then Mal said the reason she broke up with Dennis is that he beat her up a couple of times. I guess my question is, what am I getting into here? And did you already know about Mal and Dennis?"

"Answer to your first question is, you're new in town and some people are going to make it their business to find out what you're all about. I expect you've seen that before."

I had.

"And as far as your other question, Mary Alice is a good girl. But there are some people around town think she might be a little bit, what should we say, free and easy with the boys at times, if you take my meaning."

"Then, when Dennis called her a whore, was

that accurate?"

"I don't believe so," he said. "I'll just leave it at this. Mary Alice is a very pretty girl, and lots of the boys are attracted to her. Goldenrod is like every other small town. People get jealous and they talk. Sometimes they get the story right, other times not. Best thing is not to get involved until you're sure you know what's going on. That way, when the fur starts to fly, at least you'll know all the facts."

When I didn't say anything to that, Grandpa raised his eyebrows. "You didn't, did you? Get involved, I mean?"

"No." But I didn't tell him that if Robbie had not gotten between Dennis and me, the fur definitely would have started flying. And no matter who won the fight, things would not have worked out well for me.

"Then if you weren't out there mixing it up with some kid you just met, what did you do with the rest of the afternoon? Roberta said you went straight up to your room after you and Mary Alice got back."

"I wrote a letter to this girl I know back in Fresno. Her name is Laura. She asked me to write and tell her where I was staying. I think maybe she's going to send me some cookies or something."

"Is she special?" Grandpa asked.

"I guess I'd like her to be, but as much as we move around . . .."

"It's hard sometimes, isn't it? Being in service can be tough on families. Come on, let's stack these dishes in the sink and put away the leftovers. Roberta can clean up the rest when she comes tomorrow."

"It's okay, Grandpa. I can wash the dishes. I do that at home to help Mom."

I had just finished running water in the sink and setting up the dish drainer when the telephone rang.

"Hello," I heard Grandpa pick up in his study. "Yes, this is Harold Evans. Yes, I'll accept the charges." Then he called to me, "Connor, pick up the phone in the kitchen. It's your mother. Hurry up!"

I almost pulled the phone off the wall when I grabbed the receiver. "Mom?" I shouted. "Mom?"

"Just a second," I heard Grandpa say. "The operator has to put the call through."

There was a noise like sandpaper rubbing on a piece of wood. I knew that was static from the satellite relay. Then the operator said, "Go ahead, please," and I heard Mom say, "Dad, are you there?"

"I'm here, Maddie. Connor is on the extension."

"Hi, sweetie," she said. "How was the train ride?"

"Long and boring. A couple of Army officers bought me breakfast the first morning. After that, I just sat and looked out the window. Arizona and New Mexico look pretty much like California except it doesn't seem like anybody actually lives there."

She laughed, and I thought it was good to hear. She hadn't laughed much since we got the news about Dad. "How are you and Connor getting along, Dad? Is he giving you any trouble?"

"Not yet, but it's only been one day. If he gets all wild and wooly, I still have that paddle I used on your brothers around here somewhere."

I said, "Where are you, Mom?"

"I'm at the Naval Air Station at Atsugi, Japan. I just got off the transport flight and wanted to call first thing. Soon as we're finished talking here, I'm on my way to Tokyo."

"What time is it there?" I asked

"It's just after nine o'clock in the morning. We're fourteen hours ahead of you."

"Then it's tomorrow where you are?"

"Yes. It's Thursday morning."

"Mom," I said, "have you heard anything?"

"No, Connor, I don't have anything definite. I spoke to a representative from the Red Cross before we took off from San Francisco. As you might imagine, the North Vietnamese aren't in a very cooperative mood, so the Red Cross wasn't able to get any information other than to confirm the plane was shot down."

"Then Dad and Ensign Taney could be hiding in the countryside somewhere trying to make their way back."

"We don't know," Mom said. "We hope so. Right now, that's all we can do."

We didn't talk long after that. Mom said she had to get aboard a Marine helicopter that was waiting to take her from the airfield to the hospital in Tokyo, but that she'd call again when she got settled. After we hung up, Grandpa asked me if I was okay, or if there was anything about Mom what Mom said that I wanted to talk to him about. I told him thanks, but no. Then I finished washing the dishes and went upstairs to my room.

CHAPTER SIXTEEN

On Saturday morning Grandpa drove me to the post office to mail my letter and then to the park where we arrived a little after nine. A couple of the other guys on the team were already there, tossing a ball around in the outfield. I remembered one of them was our first baseman, who called himself Junior. I didn't remember the other player's name, but watching him move, I guessed he was an outfielder. When they saw Grandpa and me walking down toward the dugout, Junior motioned for me to join him and the other player where they were warming up.

"Junior Hanks," he reminded me. "This here," he said, motioning to the other player, "is Larry Griggs, in case you forgot. He's our center fielder. Why don't you go stand over there?" he said, pointing to a spot about thirty yards away. We played three-corner catch until more of the team showed up. When Robbie and Mr. Curtis drove up, we jogged back to the dugout.

"Got you a uniform, Connor," he said, and I had to admit, it was pretty cool. The shirt and the pants were white, trimmed with an orange stripe down the sides of the shirt and the pant legs, and a big orange "G" on the front of the shirt. The stirrups were orange, and the cap was black with an orange snake, obviously meant to be a copperhead (though I had never actually seen a real one) coiled into the shape of a "G." A black number 15, my number was on the back.

"You can change in the men's restroom, over there," Mr. Curtis said, pointing.

By the time I got changed, the rest of the team had showed up. Mister Curtis sent us into the field and started hitting infield and outfield practice balls. At ten o'clock he called us in so the other team, which had arrived together in a school bus, could take their warm-ups. At ten-thirty, the umpires called Mr. Curtis and the other team's coach out to home plate to hand in lineup cards and go over the ground rules. By that time, there was a pretty fair crowd filling the bleachers along the foul lines, which told me that on a Saturday morning in a small town in Kansas, there wasn't a lot to do besides watch sandlot baseball. The Caldwell Cowpokes, as they were called, brought a few fans of their own, and by the time Conrad Schmidt threw his first pitch, there wasn't an open seat to be found.

From the get-go, I knew it was going to be a long day. The Cowpokes were 0-for-the-season, but they clearly had shined up their hitting shoes today. Their leadoff man smacked Conrad's third pitch just fair down the right field line, and by the time Dennis Smith caught up with the ball and fired it back to the cutoff man, the runner was standing on third base. The next man hit a slow dribbler toward short, and instead of taking the sure out, Andy Roselli tried to nail the runner at home. His throw was high, and the ball sailed to the backstop. The runner from third scored easily and the hitter wound up at second on the error. Before the inning was over, we were down 4-0.

The Cowpokes pitcher, who did not appear to throw hard enough to break a windowpane, set our guys down in the first, 1-2-3. In the second, the 'Pokes scored two more and by the time Dennis Smith came up to bat in our half of the inning, it was 6-0. Dennis lined a double to left center but ended up stranded there as our hitters couldn't figure out what to do with the slow junk the Caldwell pitcher was serving up.

I remembered that although our league was not part of an officially sanctioned organization, we generally followed the rules set down for American Legion baseball, which, just like at home, limited pitchers to ninety pitches before they have to come out. Conrad didn't get that far. Mister Curtis asked me to chart pitches today, and by the time I had logged fifty, Mr. Curtis had seen enough.

"Time," he called to the plate umpire and walked to the mound to fetch Conrad. Johnny Melendez did a decent job of keeping things from getting too much worse. We got a few runs, and by the end of the sixth, Caldwell was leading 9-3.

"Hey, Connor," Mr. Curtis called to me when our guys came in for the bottom of the sixth, "want to finish her up?"

"Sure," I said, and while our guys batted in the home half, Dave Simon, our backup catcher, caught me while I got loose. By the time the inning was over, six of our guys had batted, and so by the time I took the mound, it was 9-5.

The first batter I faced was Number Nine, the Cowpokes third baseman, a tall right-handed hitter who was having a big day, 3-for-3, including a double. As he took his stance, I noticed he was leaning pretty far in. Robbie called for heat and patted the inside of his right thigh. I nodded and threw a fastball, high and inside, just close enough to let him know we were paying attention. He jumped out of the way so quickly that he ended up on his butt in the dirt. Ball one.

"Hey!" he called out, and his coach jumped up off his bench, but didn't say anything.

Number Nine stepped back into the box and again crowded the plate, closer this time. Robbie called for the same pitch in the same location. I gave it to him, and the batter hit the deck a second time. The Cowpokes coach was on his feet again, and this time he yelled something to the umpire about me being a headhunter, but the ump ignored him.

The next pitch was at the hitter's knees over the outside corner. He practically screwed himself into the ground swinging at it and ended up rolling it easily down the first base line. Junior Hanks barely had to move to field it and step on the bag. One down.

Their next man worked me to a 3-2 count before swinging at ball four in the dirt and striking out. Two down. The third hitter I faced lifted a high popup on a 1-2 pitch into foul territory, which Robbie caught easily. Nothing to it, inning over. We made a little noise in the bottom of the seventh, with Robbie and Dennis both driving in runs before they shut us down and the game ended 9-7.

CHAPTER SEVENTEEN

I was drying off from my post-game shower when the telephone rang. Grandpa answered and then called up the stairs that it was Mal, for me. When I picked up, she said, "Don't forget there's a party tonight at Louise's. I'll scoop you up at seven-thirty if that works for you."

"I don't know," I said. "I was kind of thinking maybe I wouldn't go."

"Sure, you're going. How do you expect to meet any new people if all you do is mope around your grandfather's house?"

"I'm only here until the end of the summer. I don't see a problem moping until then. I don't need to go to any parties."

"Right, good idea," she said. "Seven-thirty. Be ready." And she hung up.

As it turned out, the party at Louise's house attracted a crowd like it was a pep rally before a football game. I estimated at least fifty kids, half of whom Mal told me had not been invited, including a few who did not even live in Goldenrod. I recognized some of the guys from the baseball team, including Dennis and Robbie, plus Dave Simon and Conrad Schmidt. Some of the kids were smoking, and a few were drinking beer. Looking at the faces, I also guessed I was at least a year younger than most of them.

Louise lived in a big house with a big yard in a subdivision where every house seemed to be two or three times the size of our rental house back in Fresno. The party was well underway by the time Mal and I got there. There were cars parked up and down the street and bumper-to-bumper in the driveway, so we had to leave the Crapmobile about halfway down the block and walk back to the house.

The party was in the back yard, where there was a covered patio and lots of lawn furniture. A portable stereo had been set up and one kid whom I did not know had assigned himself the job of disc jockey, with the intent, it seemed, of finding out how loud he could make the music before the speakers cracked. He played some Beach Boys and Beatles oldies and some country songs like "Folsom Prison Blues," by Johnny Cash, and "Stand by Your Man," by Tammy Wynette. When he played an old slow song called "Blue Velvet," some of the kids got up and danced and a few started making out right in the middle of the song. About the time the song ended Robbie wandered over to the picnic bench where I was sitting with Mal. To my surprise, he was smoking.

"Take a hit?" He held out a narrow cigarette rolled in yellow paper.

I looked over at Mal. She gave an almost

imperceptible head shake. That was my cue. "Not tonight, but thanks."

How 'bout a beer, then?" he asked, and without waiting for an answer handed me a brown bottle.

I had been to a few parties back in California where kids brought liquor, but they were always careful not to let any of the parents find out about it. Nobody at this party seemed to be worried about that, though, and it wasn't long before I found out Louise's parents had gone to Oklahoma City for the weekend and didn't even know there was a party. I also learned that in Kansas it was legal to drink beer at age eighteen, so if you had an older brother or sister, or were on good terms with a friendly Seven-Eleven store clerk, buying beer was as simple as slapping your money down on the counter.

I wasn't quite sure about the beer, but this time Mal knew what she wanted to do. She took the bottle from Robbie and drank half the contents in a single swallow. Then she passed what was left to me.

"Go ahead and finish it. It won't kill you."

I hesitated at first and then thought well, why not, and gulped down what was left. Robbie was apparently keeping an eye on us because we had no sooner finished the beer when he brought us each another bottle. I had a feeling that this was going to lead to trouble, but then decided, the hell with it, nobody was going to find out about it, anyway, and took it. After that, things seemed go sideways in a hurry, and after a few more beers I was feeling a little bit dizzy. I looked at my watch: nine fifty-five. We had been at the party just about two hours and had consumed four bottles of beer apiece, plus the first one we'd split right after we first got there. During that time, we talked a little. Mal said that when she finished high school, she wanted to go to Wichita State and work toward a degree, either as a veterinarian, like her father, or as a nurse.

"Otherwise, I'll wind up stuck here in Goldenrod and end up married to one of these guys like the ones you've already met. Next thing, I'll have a bunch of kids and then I'll really be screwed."

"You make all that sound like a bad thing."

"I can't imagine anything worse. You know, we have a saying that Goldenrod's main export is people, and unless your family owns a business or a farm, there's not much reason to stay here. How about you? Do you want to be a pilot like your dad?"

"I don't think so," I said. "I took a flying lesson once. I got it as a birthday present last year.

It wasn't a Phantom like my father is assigned to, it was just a Cessna. That's a plane for beginners when they're first learning to fly. Anyhow, Dad and I took it up and, to tell you the truth, I was more interested in looking out the window than I was flying the plane. It was interesting seeing some of the places my friends and I hang out from the air, but actually flying the plane didn't grab me. I never took another lesson."

"So, what then?"

"I'm thinking I'd like to be a doctor, like my mom. I mean, I get what my dad does, and I understand he's following orders and serving the country. He's a good man, but I think I'd feel better helping people get well than I would dropping bombs on them."

"Sensible, but that's a lot of school. You up for that?"

"Well, I've got three more years of high school and then . . .."

"Wait," she cut me off. "You're only going to be a soph? You're almost the same age as me, and I'm going to be a junior. Did you flunk something?"

"No. When I was little, we were moving a lot because of the Navy, so I started school a year late. That means I'm almost a year older than everybody in my class, but I'm a year behind where

I should be."

Then she asked me about California, and I explained that where we lived in the Central Valley looked more like Kansas than what she had probably seen on television.

"What about surfing?" she wanted to know. "Have you ever been surfing?"

"That's mostly in the movies and records by the Beach Boys," I told her. "We don't live anywhere near the ocean, so I've never been surfing and I don't know anybody who has." But when she asked me about Dad and whether I thought he'd be okay she saw very quickly that I was having trouble talking about it and let it drop.

After a while I noticed that some of the couples who had arrived together, or who had connected after showing up with other kids had begun to wander off, either into the house or back toward the front where the cars were parked. It didn't take much imagination to figure out what that was all about. Mal noticed it, too. It gave her an idea.

"Hey," she said, "you want to go someplace a little more private? Maybe we could get to know each other a little better? I know a couple of spots where nobody will bother us."

Right. Grandpa had said that some people thought Mal could sometimes be "free and easy," as he put it, around boys, and I was pretty sure I knew what he was talking about. I was even more sure that whatever Mal had in mind was a bad idea, but the beer we had been drinking let me get past that, no problem. And that's why, when she held out her hand to me and said, "Come on, let's go," I took it and said, "Okay."

Once back in the Crapmobile, Mal started the engine and started driving down the road heading back toward town. We hadn't gone more than a mile or so when we saw in the distance red flashing lights approaching from the direction in which we were heading. Mal quickly pulled into the next driveway we came to and killed the lights.

Then as we watched, two sheriff's department cars flew past us and went speeding down the road toward Louise's house. We were too far away to see what happened after that, and when I suggested to Mal that we go back and take a look, she said, "Are you goofy? We need to get out of here now."

It wasn't until the next day that we found out that a neighbor who knew Louise's parents were out of town heard all the noise coming from her house and, guessing what was going on, called the sheriff. The two cars that passed us blocked the road on either side of Louise's house and then the deputies broke up the party, but not before getting the names and addresses of everybody there. Then they radioed the names back to their headquarters, after which each of the kids' parents got a telephone call. The parents of the ones who had obviously been drinking had to come get them, and every single kid was cited for disturbing the peace. The few whose parents couldn't be reached, including Louise, were taken to the sheriff's station and held there until a relative came to pick them up.

CHAPTER EIGHTEEN

It was about eleven o'clock when Mal dropped me at Grandpa's house. I could tell from the dark window in his bedroom that he had already gone to bed, so I let myself in with the key he had given me and went upstairs as quietly as I could. After what had happened at Louise's party, I had a suspicion that Grandpa's telephone would be ringing first thing Sunday morning, and that he wouldn't be happy to hear what the caller had to say.

Sure enough, the call came at five minutes past nine.

I could hear Grandpa's voice coming from the kitchen, but I couldn't quite make out what he was saying. However, I was sure that the caller was somebody from the sheriff's department, and I was just as sure that soon after he hung up, he would be calling me downstairs. The summons wasn't long in coming.

"Connor," he called from the foot of the stairs, "are you up?"

"Yes, Grandpa, I was just getting ready to take a shower."

"Come down here first. I need to talk to you."

While I was pulling on a pair of jeans and a

t-shirt, I heard Grandpa coughing, like he had gotten something stuck in his throat. By the time I got downstairs, the coughing had stopped and he was sitting at the kitchen table with a cup of coffee in front of him. He was dressed in a shirt and tie, as if he were set to go to work at the courthouse. The Sunday paper was laying off to one side. I supposed he had been reading it when the phone rang.

"Sit down, Connor," he said. "Want some coffee?"

I sat. "No, thanks."

"You all right, boy?" he said, looking at me the way a person might size up a used car before making an offer to buy it. "You have a bad night?"

"I didn't sleep very well, I guess."

"Hard to be your best when you toss and turn all night." He took a sip of his coffee. "Tell me about the party last night."

"The party?"

"The party you and Mary Alice went to last night at that Porter girl's house. You did go to that party, didn't you?"

"Yes."

"Well, what went on? And before you say anything, you might want to remember, a good lawyer never asks a question he doesn't already know the answer to."

"I'm not sure what I can tell you," I said,

"Mal—I'm sorry, Mary Alice—picked me up in her mom's car about seven-thirty. We were there a couple of hours, and then we left."

"How come so early? Weren't you having any fun?"

"There were a lot of people there that I didn't know."

"I see." He looked at me, hard. "Why don't we just save a lot of time and lay our cards on the table here, Connor? I expect you already figured out that was the sheriff called me this morning."

"I guess."

"And you probably know what he wanted to talk to me about."

I had a choice here. I could play dumb and act like I didn't know what he was talking about, or I could, as he said, lay my cards on the table. Since I wasn't sure what he already knew, I figured that might be the safest bet.

"When Mary Alice and I were leaving, we saw a couple of sheriff's cars heading toward Louise's house. We thought somebody must have complained about the noise."

"The noise, yes, that's right, and as it also turned out, the underage drinking and the fact that all this was going on while that girl's parents were in Oklahoma City. The deputies rounded up thirty-seven youngsters and held them there until their parents could come and get them. Couple of 'em ended up spending the night in protective custody at the jail before the deputies could find somebody to come and take them home.

"They threw them into jail?" I asked.

"No. They sat 'em down in the break room in the courthouse to wait for their ride home. First question for you is, did you know her parents were out of town?"

"I didn't before we got there, but it was obvious after a while. I mean it got really noisy and there were a lot of kids there that Mal told me Louise hadn't invited. It seemed like if her mom and dad were home, they would have come outside to find out why there were so many more people there than what there should have been."

"How about the drinking, did you know about that?"

This time I couldn't look him in the eye. "Not until we got there. I didn't know ahead of time."

"Uh-huh. How much did you have?"

"I don't know. Maybe a couple of beers."

I knew he didn't a hundred percent believe me, but he let it pass. He also didn't ask about the marijuana, so maybe that got ditched before the deputies showed up.

"Okay, just one more thing, and this is

important. You said you had a few beers. Did you and Mary Alice do anything after you left the party that might come back to bite you later on?"

This time I looked straight at him. "No, sir, we did not. After we left Louise's house, Mal drove me straight back here. Far as I know, after that, she went home."

"All right, then," he said, and got up from the table. "I've got to go into town and have a sit-down with the court clerk."

What the hell just happened here? I thought.

"You have to work on Sunday?"

"We got ourselves thirty-seven juvenile offenders. We got to figure out a hearing date for them and their folks, and then we got to get set up to send out summonses. It's going to take some time, so I'll probably be gone until this afternoon. You think you can find yourself something to eat if I'm not back by lunchtime?"

I told him I'd be fine, and that I wasn't very hungry anyway. Then I noticed something I hadn't seen earlier. "Grandpa? There's something on your shirt, right there next to your tie. It looks like blood."

He looked at the spot. "It isn't anything. I must've nicked myself shaving this morning."

"Okay," I said, but I wondered: *Who shaves in the morning wearing a shirt and tie?*

CHAPTER NINETEEN

When Grandpa got back from his meeting with the court clerk, he went straight to his bedroom to take a nap, he said, and sure enough, in a in a few minutes I heard him snoring. That left me on my own for a few hours, and I killed the time watching a baseball game on television. After that, I went outside and sat in the big glider swing Grandpa kept on the porch. It was a hot day, and very still, and it got me thinking about how hot it must be in Vietnam and what Dad was experiencing if he was trying to make his way through the jungle back to safety. That is, if he survived the plane crash.

And then I got scared. What if he didn't make it? What would Mom and I do, and what if we had to keep moving around? What if she got reassigned back to the hospital in Japan after the end of August? Would I have to move to Tokyo to be with Mom, or would I have to stay here in Kansas with Grandpa and a bunch of people I barely knew for God knows how long?

The sun was beginning to drop low in the sky when I heard Grandpa stirring around. He was coughing again, and I wondered how long that had been going on. Maybe it was just a summer cold, I thought, and he'd get over it in a few days.

I heard him clear his throat. "Connor?"

"On the porch, Grandpa."

The screen door banged shut behind him. "Ready for some supper?"

Since nobody had prepared anything we ended up at the same diner in town where we had lunch the day that he met me at the train. During the drive into town, and all during our meal, I expected to get a "talking-to" about last night's party, but it never came up, and neither did he say anything about what was going to happen to the kids taken into police custody that night. Instead, he asked me what I had been doing all day. I told him I had watched a ball game on television and then reminded him the Copperheads had a practice on Tuesday night and an away game on Wednesday night against some team from just over the border in Blackwell, Oklahoma.

"I'll be sure to be there," he promised. Then he asked me when my sixteenth birthday would be.

"Couple months," I told him. "August second."

"Well, if you want, we could fix you up with some driving lessons and then you could get your license here in Kansas. Least then, you wouldn't need me or Mary Alice running you around everywhere you need to go."

"I don't live in Kansas, Grandpa," I said. "I live in California."

"Not now, you don't. For the time being, you live in Kansas, and since I know all the folks down at the license bureau, nobody there is going to put up much of a fuss about your place of residence. When you get back home, you can turn in your Kansas license and get a California license without having to take a test all over again. That is, unless you'd rather use this old bicycle I got hanging in the garage. We can have that old girl fixed up in a day or two."

"Oh, hell no," I almost shouted, and then braced for an immediate "Watch your language," but instead Grandpa just grinned and said, "Then we can start your lessons later this week. I have to run an errand tomorrow, and then we'll see if we can get you going."

Grandpa's errand must have been an early one because he was up and out of the house about the time the sun was coming up. When I heard him start up the big Cadillac, I went to the window and watched as he headed down the road. Knowing I had the house to myself for the next several hours, I climbed back into bed and slept another couple of hours. Then I showered and went downstairs to see whether I could find something I could eat for breakfast. I didn't need much, just enough to tide me over until Mal and her mom showed up. I ended up toasting a couple slices of bread which I spread with peanut butter. That plus a glass of orange juice quieted the rumble in my stomach. And then I thought about Mrs. Mueller and what she might have to say about Mal and me at the party on Saturday night. It was true we were gone before the sheriff's deputies showed up, but in a town the size of Goldenrod, there was no way she wouldn't have heard about it by now.

Maybe that talking-to was still to come.

CHAPTER TWENTY

Mal and her mom showed up at the house around eleven-thirty. Mrs. Mueller seemed a little chillier than other times, so there was no doubt she had already heard the worst about Saturday night. She asked me if I wanted her to fix me some lunch, and when I told her I was good, she said, "Suit yourself," and began bustling around, cleaning the kitchen. Mal was dispatched to the hall closet where the vacuum cleaner was kept and told to get busy in the dining room. Since there was nothing else for me to do, I went out to the garage to take a look at the bicycle Grandpa had talked about the day before.

I found it hanging on hooks attached to the back wall. It was an old Schwinn Black Phantom, painted, not surprisingly, black with red and silver trim. It had wide whitewall balloon tires and coaster brakes. And it was heavy. It took me a couple of tries to lift it down off the wall for a closer inspection. Apart from having two flat tires and being incredibly dusty, it appeared to be in good shape. I rolled it out into the yard and then turned it upside down so that it rested on its handlebars and seat. I began turning the pedals by hand, and after I got it going, it looked like there was nothing wrong that a few squirts of oil wouldn't fix. When I pushed the pedal in the opposite direction, the back wheel slowed and then stopped. That meant the coaster brake still worked.

I dug a couple of shop rags out of a box in the garage and used the hose to wet them. I spent the next half-hour wiping the bike down, and when I turned it right side up and set it on its flat tires, it looked pretty good. I was looking around in the garage for a tire pump when Mal found me.

"My mom is pretty pissed," she said. "You might have noticed when we came in."

"Pissed at you, or pissed at me?"

"Both of us, but mostly me. You get a partial pass because you're new here, you weren't driving and, strictly speaking, it was me who invited you."

"Actually, it was Louise who invited both of us."

"Yeah, well, Mom doesn't know that. What she does know is that I came home smelling like beer. I managed to convince her somebody spilled it on me, and lucky for me, she bought it. But then that just got us back to her wanting to know what we were doing at a party where there was drinking going on. If she thought I actually had something to drink, I'd be grounded with no Crapmobile privileges until I turned thirty. So if she asks you any questions about what happened, I need you to back me up."

"Got it."

"One other thing." She paused for a moment, as if gathering her thoughts. "About Saturday night. I know what I said about going someplace private when we left, but I want you to understand we weren't going to get it all in."

"What are you talking about?"

"Connor, my dad is a veterinarian, okay? I've seen calves born and chickens hatched. I know where babies come from and I'm not ready for that."

"Well, my mother is a doctor, and I think I could deliver a baby if I had to. I'm pretty sure I'm not ready for that, either."

"Then we understand each other." She put her arms around my neck, pulled me close and kissed me hard, on the lips. "That's what you missed because we had to lay low until the cops were gone. And we'll be able to get some more of that in if you don't turn out to be a jerk, like most of these guys around here."

"And if I don't, then what?"

"Listen, you're a cute guy. A little slow sometimes, but even so, I like you, maybe even a lot. And I don't know what you thought was going to happen, or what you're hoping is going to happen, but there is no way we're going to hop in the back seat of a car and make a baby."

"I never thought . . .." I began.

"Look, Connor, I told you about how it went with Denny and me, and as bad as that might have sounded to you, he's really not that different from any of the other boys around here. You saw what was starting to happen at Louise's party. If the cops hadn't showed up when they did, it would have turned into a huge make-out session and somebody would have ended up in serious trouble. It's happened before.

She shook her head. "That's not what I want for myself. I already told you I'm planning on going to college, and I can't do that if I let some guy get me into trouble, even if he is sweet and comes from California with blond hair and a killer tan. You understand?"

I started to say something, but she held up her hand like a crossing guard with a stop sign. "Yes or no?"

"Yes."

"Okay, good, then we're still friends. And besides," she said, turning to go back into the house, "I heard a rumor you've got a girlfriend back in California. I'm not getting into the middle of that."

CHAPTER TWENTY-ONE

Grandpa got home at five-thirty, just about the time Mal and Mrs. Mueller were heading home for the evening. "I left supper for you and Connor in the oven, Judge. I made your favorite, fried chicken with scalloped potatoes and green beans. There's some corn bread, too. You can warm it in the toaster oven for a minute or so if you want."

"I thank you," he said. "I had a long day today and I'm a bit tired, so if I don't eat all you made, don't think I didn't like it."

"I also made a list of things you're running low on. I'll stop at the store in the morning and pick them up. I'll make sure to leave you the receipt."

After they were gone, he said to me, "Connor, I'm going to lay down for a few minutes. If you get hungry, go ahead and eat. You don't need to wait for me.

"Okay, Grandpa. You want me to wake you up later?"

"No," he said. "Just let me sleep."

I heard him go into his room and shut the door, and then I heard him start coughing again. I thought about knocking on his door to ask if there was anything wrong and then decided not to. I figured, if there was something that he wanted to tell me, he'd get around to it when he was ready.

Until then, I'd mind my own business.

I ate the supper Mrs. Mueller had left for me, and since it didn't look as though Grandpa would be coming out of his bedroom, I covered his plate in foil and put it in the refrigerator. Then I went into the living room and watched television. When the ten o'clock news came on, the lead story was, as it seemed to be every night now, the war in Vietnam. Lately the military had taken to reporting body counts, which is the total of Viet Cong and North Vietnamese regular army personnel killed by U. S. forces. The idea seemed to be that if our Army and Marines finally killed or captured every last enemy fighter, then the war would be over.

The other main story was the Democratic Party's California presidential primary election, which was to take place the next day. I remembered before I left seeing yard signs all around Fresno, indicating support for various candidates, including Vice President Hubert Humphrey, Minnesota Senator Eugene McCarthy and New York Senator Robert Kennedy, the younger brother of former President John F. Kennedy. The reason the primary election meant anything at all was that President Lyndon Johnson had announced in April that, because of the growing unpopularity of the war, he would not seek re-election in November.

I watched the weather report and then the

baseball scores. The Giants were playing the Philadelphia Phillies at home, and the Dodgers were in Los Angeles against the Pirates, but since it was only eight-thirty in California, there were no final scores. I turned off the television and went upstairs to my room. I fell asleep thinking about the war and wondering what were the chances I would ever see my father again.

When I came downstairs the next morning, Grandpa was sitting at the kitchen table drinking a cup of coffee and reading the morning newspaper.

"Morning, Connor," he said, looking up. "Want some coffee?"

"I think just some orange juice, thanks."

"You know where to find it," he said, and went back to reading his newspaper.

I retrieved the OJ from the refrigerator, poured a glass and sat down across the table from Grandpa.

"Want part of the paper?"

"No. I watched the news last night. It's all about the war and the election in California. I doubt it's anything different this morning."

"You know," Grandpa said, putting down the paper, "that Kennedy fellow is expected to win in California. If he does, the Democrats will likely make him their candidate in the fall. He says the first thing he'll do is get the war over."

"I hope he does," I said. I took a drink of my orange juice. "Grandpa, can I ask you something? It's kind of personal."

"Well, then I'll have to be as careful answering as you'll be asking."

"Well, it's just that . . . it's just that, since I've been here, you've been coughing a lot, and I don't think that spot on your shirt the other day came from a shaving cut."

"You think there's something wrong with me and you want to know what it is?"

"I want to be sure that you're okay."

"Well, I can tell you this much. I saw the doctor yesterday. Had to go all the way to Wichita for that. That's why I left early. He ran some tests and said he'd let me know in a day or two, so right now I can't tell you what's going on with me. Meantime, I'll make you a promise. When the doctor tells me more, I'll tell you. Until then, I don't want you worrying about me. Is that a deal?"

After that, Grandpa went to work at the courthouse. I spent the morning cutting the lawn, mostly to kill time until Mal and her mother showed up to take care of Grandpa's housework. I was looking forward to seeing Mal, but as it turned out, Mrs. Mueller came by herself. She said Mal had something else to do that day, so I was stuck by myself until suppertime.

Having nothing better to do, I took out the bicycle I had cleaned up, pumped air into the tires and took off down the road, heading away from town. I must have ridden for ten miles or more, up and down county roads. It was fairly easy going, since the landscape around that part of Kansas was pretty flat, and as I rode past what seemed like an endless vista of corn and wheatfields, I began to gain an appreciation for a part of the country that I had never thought much about before. In truth, I thought, except for there being no palm trees, southern Kansas didn't look much different from the part of California where we lived.

Grandpa and I ate our evening meal together and then it was time for baseball practice. We were three players short that evening, as Dave Beatty, Dennis Smith and Conrad Schmidt were all missing. It wasn't hard to guess why, since all three of them were at the party on Saturday night. I was surprised, though, to see that Robbie Curtis was there with his dad. Since I had already knew his dad had kind of a short fuse, I figured if Robbie did come to practice, he might show up with another black eye. But no, he was there as if nothing at all had happened.

When I asked him about it, he said, "When I saw the cop cars coming, I lit out running through Louise's back yard and hid in the woods until everybody was gone."

I remembered that Grandpa had told Robbie that he couldn't drive except to go to work and back. And since Robbie's car was parked safely in front of his own house and not Louise's, the deputies didn't have any clue Robbie was even there.

"I had to walk home, but my folks are used to me staying out late on the weekends, so they didn't say anything about what time I got home. They heard about the party Sunday morning at church, but I told 'em I wasn't there, and unless somebody rats me out, they'll never know any different."

"They won't hear it from me," I said. I wanted to ask him if he thought the parents of the guys who were missing from practice might make them sit out the game on Wednesday night, but Mr. Curtis called Robbie and me over to the dugout.

"Connor, maybe Robbie didn't tell you about this, but we have a rule. If you don't come to practice, you don't start, so unless Conrad is hiding out here someplace and I'm not seeing him, I'm going to start you tomorrow night against the Bulldogs. Think you can handle that?"

"I guess so, sure, why not?"

"Okay, then. We played them last year, and they're a bunch of hitting fools. I don't want you to do anything tonight except some running in the outfield and maybe throw a few soft tosses with Robbie here, 'cause you're gonna need your good stuff when you face these guys."

I groaned inwardly at that. After a two-hour bike ride earlier in the day, I thought running was probably the last thing I needed to do, but I decided not to bring it up.

"I'll do my best," I said, but in fact I never had the chance to throw so much as a single pitch on Wednesday, because something happened on Tuesday night that made a baseball game between two small-town traveling teams seem not very important at all.

CHAPTER TWENTY-TWO

Maybe it was sleeping in a bed other than my own, or maybe it was being in a time zone two hours different from home, but since I'd moved into Grandpa's upstairs bedroom, I found myself most days waking up at a much earlier hour than usual. When I rolled over and looked at the clock the next morning, it read 5:45. Not nearly time to get out of bed, either in Kansas or in California, and yet it was light outside and I was wide awake with my stomach growling and no hope of getting back to sleep.

Quietly, so I wouldn't wake Grandpa, I got dressed and went downstairs to see if I could find something to eat. Scrounging in the refrigerator, I came up with some orange juice and a leftover chicken leg from the supper Mrs. Mueller had cooked a couple of nights earlier. Then I went into the living room and turned on the television. This early in the morning, the only thing I could find to watch was the news, but since it was that or nothing, I sat down on the couch to see what was going on in the world. I expected to hear about weather or the war in Vietnam, but what I got was something quite different.

In a somber voice, a network announcer was explaining that shortly after midnight California time, Robert Kennedy had been shot and wounded following his primary election victory celebration at a hotel in Los Angeles. The film footage that accompanied the announcement showed Senator Kennedy leaving the ballroom of the hotel through the kitchen, where he was confronted by a gunman who shot him once in the head and twice in the right shoulder. In the struggle to subdue the gunman, five other people were wounded. The announcer said Senator Kennedy was rushed to a nearby hospital, where he underwent emergency surgery. The shooter was identified as a Jordanian national named Sirhan Sirhan, who was reportedly unhappy with Senator Kennedy's outspoken support for Israel.

As I sat watching, I realized that Grandpa had come out of his bedroom and was standing behind me.

"My, God," he said, not again."

I turned and saw the stricken look on his face. "Grandpa, how does this keep happening?"

Just two months earlier, civil rights leader Martin Luther King had been shot and killed by an assassin at a hotel in Memphis, Tennessee. And although I was only ten years old at the time, I had a clear memory of the assassination of President John F. Kennedy in Dallas on a day in November 1963. I remembered that it happened on a Friday while we were in school, and when the announcement came over the speaker system, it was like the world had come to a complete stop as we first listened, and later watched, the news coverage of the shooting.

"I don't know," he said at last, sounding very tired. "I think there are people in this world just don't know how to be a human being." He came around to the front of the couch where I was sitting.

"Lot of things go on every day that just isn't right" He sighed and placed his hand on my shoulder for just a moment, and I could see real sadness in his eyes. "This one just touches more of us."

The news broadcasts stayed on the air for the rest of the morning, replacing the usual lineup of game shows, soap operas and re-runs of old movies. After watching for another hour or so, it looked as though the networks had nothing further to report. Senator Kennedy had survived the surgery, although nobody could say for sure whether he would recover from his wounds. The shooter was in custody, and there was no evidence to suggest that the attack on Senator Kennedy was part of a larger conspiracy.

Grandpa took a break shortly before nine o'clock to telephone his clerk at the courthouse to inform her that he would not be coming in to work today. Then he went into his room and closed the door.

At around eleven, the telephone rang.

"Is this Connor?" the voice at the other end asked when I picked up.

"Yes."

"Connor, this is Coach Curtis. I expect you and the judge have been watching the news?"

"Yes, sir," I told him. "We've been watching it on TV all morning."

"Well, it's a terrible thing, and I wanted to let you know that the situation being what it is, the game tonight has been called off. We'll try to make it up later in the season, but nobody's much in the mood to be any playin' any baseball tonight."

"I understand," I said. "I'll let Grandpa know."

"I appreciate it. Oh, and don't worry about losing your start. You come to practice on Thursday, we'll run you out there on Saturday, just like I promised."

"Thank you," I said, and hung up, not caring at that moment whether I pitched another baseball ever again.

Right after I finished talking to Coach Curtis, the phone rang again. This time it was Mrs. Mueller, wondering if I could ask Grandpa if it would be all right if she didn't come over today to clean and cook supper. She said she had been watching the news and wanted to stay with it to find out whether Senator Kennedy would be okay. I told her Grandpa was taking a nap and that he wasn't going to work today either, so I thought it wouldn't be a problem if she and Mal stayed home.

Today, it seemed as though nobody wanted to do anything.

Later in the day the news got worse, as we learned that Robert Kennedy had died. In the days that followed, his body was returned from California to New York, the state he represented in the Senate. There was a funeral mass held at St. Patrick's Cathedral, in New York City, and then his flag-draped coffin was carried by a special train to Washington, where he was buried at Arlington National Cemetery, near the grave of his brother, President John F. Kennedy.

According to news reports, somewhere between one and two million people turned out to watch the train as it passed along its route from New York to Washington.

Late Sunday afternoon, Mom called from Tokyo. Grandpa was in his room, napping, I thought, so I picked up, hoping the telephone hadn't wakened him.

Like the first time we spoke, there was a scratchy noise sound in the background that was static caused by the satellite that relayed our conversation between Japan and the United States.

"Oh, Connor," she said. "I guess you've been following the news."

"It'd be hard not to, Mom. It's all over television and we only have a few channels here."

"Are you okay? Do you need to talk about it?"

"I don't think so," I told her. "Grandpa and I have been all over it. I'm just sorry it happened in California. Do you think there'll be rioting like there was after Dr. King was shot?"

"No, I don't. The police have the man who did it. I think that will be enough, at least for a while." She stopped talking for a moment, as if she had something else that she needed to tell me but didn't quite know where to start. I decided to give her a push.

"Did you hear something about Dad? Is that why you're calling?"

"It is, partly," she said, after a moment. "But I'm afraid there is still no news. Not from the Red Cross, not from the Swiss and not from the North Vietnamese. At this point, we just simply don't know what happened after he ejected or where he is now."

"So that's it, then, isn't it?"

"I choose not to believe that Connor, and

you should, too. I keep telling myself that somehow he managed to get away, and that he's hiding, or he's been taken in by friendlies, until they can find a way to move him to safety."

When I didn't say anything, she said, "I need you to tell me you believe that, too, Connor. Can you do that for me?"

"Sure, Mom, if it will make you feel better, I believe that. I really do."

"Okay," she said. "Hang on to that. Now, I need to talk to your Grandfather, but I also wanted to ask you how you're getting along. Have you made any friends yet?"

So, I told her about playing baseball, and about Mal and her mother, and Robbie, and that I got invited to a party. But I didn't tell her about the sheriff arresting thirty-seven kids at that party, or that I had been drinking beer, or that Grandpa was going to start giving me driving lessons. I figured she didn't need anything else to worry about. But there was one more thing I wanted her to know.

"Mom, before you talk to Grandpa, I should tell you, he's been coughing a lot. It's not like when somebody has a cold. It's way worse than that. I don't know how long it's been going on, but I noticed it almost as soon as I got here."

"Yes, well, I grew up in that part of the country. This time of year, there's a lot of dust in the air on account of there's a lot of plowed ground and it gets windy. It's probably just an allergic reaction. I wouldn't worry about it."

I said, "He's coughing up blood, Mom. He went to a doctor in Wichita the other day. He said they were running some tests. I don't know if he's heard anything yet."

"Okay," she said. "Go find him and tell him I called and I need to talk to him. And Connor? I love you, and no matter how all this turns out, we'll be okay. Remember that. We're going to be okay.

CHAPTER TWENTY-THREE

On Monday when he got back from work, Grandpa said he had two big announcements for me. The first one was that that evening after supper he would be giving me my first driving lesson in his Cadillac.

"Now, Connor," he told me, "I don't want you to be nervous or anything, but this car cost just over six thousand dollars."

Right, don't be nervous. But what if I put this tub in the ditch in the first ten minutes?

"What's the other thing?"

"On Thursday morning, we're going to have a little get-together over at the courthouse with all those kids who got picked up at that party last week. Well, them and their folks, I should say. I thought it might be a good idea if you and Mary Alice came along, maybe just to give you an idea what you got away with, since after all, you did get away with it. I already spoke with Mrs. Mueller about it, and she thought it might do Mary Alice some good."

I felt my heart drop into my shoes. Thirty-seven kids, all of whom got caught partying, drinking, and who knows what else. And every one of them will know that not only did Mal and I not get caught, but that we would be there to see what kind of punishment Grandpa was going to hand out.

It was as if my life in Goldenrod, Kansas, didn't suck enough already. Now there would be this, and not only would it come crashing down on me, but on Mal as well.

"Oh, Grandpa," I said, "are you sure that's such a good idea? I mean, all of those kids and their parents know who Mal is, and some of them know me, and they're going to think you're letting us get away with the same thing they're being punished for."

"You two didn't get arrested. You should have, I expect, but you didn't, and that's all there is to it. Anybody doesn't like it, they can come talk to me."

After supper, I found myself sitting behind the wheel in Grandpa's Sedan Deville. Looking out through the car's wide windshield, I saw a dark blue, polished hood that seemed to stretch all the way to the horizon. From where I sat, it looked as long and as wide as the flight deck of the *Constellation* must have looked to my father when he was seated in the cockpit of his Phantom, positioned for takeoff.

The instrument panel, which I was told to familiarize myself with, was simple enough. It held a speedometer that went up to 120 miles per hour, a fuel gauge, a temperature gauge and a clock. The wide blue leather seat where I was sitting, with

Grandpa on the passenger side, could be moved up and back and tilted forward and backward with a switch. On Mom's car, and every other car I'd ever been in, if you wanted to move the seat, you pulled a lever at the bottom and used your legs to push back and forth. Same thing with the outside mirrors. In Mom's car, you had to roll down the window and move the mirror by hand. On Grandpa's car you just moved a switch in the arm rest and the mirrors would move wherever you wanted.

It only took a minute to get the seat where I could see out the windshield comfortably and reach the pedals and to buckle my seat belt. Grandpa then told me to put my foot on the brake and start the car. Then, while my foot was still on the brake, I moved the shift lever into "Drive" and we started down Grandpa's long driveway. When we got to the road, I put my foot on the brake and we made a hard stop, as if I had run straight into a solid wall.

"That's a power brake, Connor. You don't need to stomp on it to get the car to stop."

"Okay, Grandpa," I said, and sure enough, after a few more stops I got the hang of stopping the car without throwing either of us headfirst through the windshield.

We turned out of the driveway and headed out of town on the county road, where there were very few other cars to worry about. Back home, I had ridden my bike in traffic almost from the day I learned to get around on two wheels, but steering Grandpa's giant Cadillac was a different experience altogether. In fact, I didn't even come close to hitting anybody or anything, but just the same, driving a car for the first time on a public highway that I had to share with other drivers was a scary experience.

"You'll get used to it," Grandpa said after a few miles. "Turn right at the next road and then we'll swing around and head for home. For your first time, I'd say you did pretty good. Time your birthday rolls around, you'll be driving with the best of 'em."

"I hope so," I said, and actually started to feel pretty good about myself. The feeling didn't last though, because as we got close to home, Grandpa started coughing again, and he didn't stop until after we got back inside the house.

CHAPTER TWENTY-FOUR

When I came downstairs the next morning, I was surprised to see Grandpa was sitting at the kitchen table reading his newspaper. Most days, by the time I got up, he was already at work at the courthouse. Today, though, he wasn't wearing his usual dark suit and time. Instead, he was wearing khaki work pants and a short-sleeved cotton shirt.

"Morning, boy," he greeted me.

"Good morning, Grandpa. Aren't you going to work today?"

"Nothing on the calendar, so I thought I'd stick around the house today, maybe catch up on some paperwork, maybe do some gardening." He folded his newspaper carefully and laid it down on the table next to his coffee cup.

"And maybe answer one or two questions that I figure you've got for me."

"Questions, Grandpa?"

"Connor, I've been a judge in this county longer that you've been alive, and I guess in that time I've just about every shaggy dog story there ever was." When I didn't pick up on that right away, he said, "That means I know when somebody's either not telling the whole truth, part of the truth, or they're flat-out lying. So, do you want to ask your question, or should I just go ahead and tell you what's wrong with me? Because I know you told your mom about it."

"I know. I'm sorry, I shouldn't have said anything."

"No, it's all right. I would have told her anyway. I went to see a doctor last week. I had to go to Wichita, which is why I left so early. The doctor's name is Morrow. He's an oncologist. Do you know what that is?"

I nodded. "A cancer specialist. I met one once when Mom was showing me around the base hospital."

"Right. My doctor here sent me to Dr. Morrow because he wanted to be sure what we're dealing with."

He paused, gathering his thoughts. "My doctor noticed a spot on one of my lungs when I had a chest X-ray as part of my last checkup. He couldn't tell if it was what's called a pulmonary nodule, which is basically nothing, or if it was lung cancer."

"It's cancer, isn't it? That's where the blood is coming from."

"Looks that way. I'm going back to Wichita later this week for more tests, but he seems pretty sure that's what we're up against. It's one of the reasons I need you to learn how to drive. If I have to be running back and forth to Wichita for treatment,

I might not be feeling good enough after to drive myself back home, and I don't want to be spending the night up there. So, you're going to have to come along so you can run me back."

I felt myself getting wobbly in the knees. It was too much to take in. First Dad getting shot down, and for all anybody knew, killed in action. Then Mom ordered back on active duty in Japan, and now this? I said, "But Grandpa, how can it be lung cancer? You don't even smoke."

"First thing I said, too. But we live here in farm country, and there's a lot of dust in the air for half the year, and a lot of chemicals being put into the soil. That's where the dust comes from, when the farmers plow and when they harvest. Doctor Morrow thinks that might be what caused, well, this. At this point, it doesn't really matter, because, wherever it came from, we've got to take care of it, and you're going to have to be part of the treatment."

"You could move," I offered. "Go someplace where the air is cleaner."

"You mean like the mountains? People in the old days used to do that for tuberculosis. Taking the cure, they called it. The dry air sometimes helped, but this isn't that, and anyway, they've got medicines now that do the job much better. Besides, where would I move to? I've lived here my whole life and I expect to keep on living here for at least a while longer."

"So then, there's nothing we can do?"

"Well, it's not going to fix itself, if that's what you mean. But let's just hang on and see what the doctor has to say when I go back later in the week."

That afternoon I was sitting on the front porch with Mal. I told her about my conversation with Grandpa, and that I was really worried. She took my hand in both of hers and held it tight.

"It's going to be okay. Your grandfather has been the judge in this part of the county as long as anybody can remember, and he's not going anywhere any time soon. He's as tough as they come, and he'll get through this. Besides, you said his doctor told him it might be nothing more than, what did he call it, a nodule? That's not a bad thing, is it?"

"Mal, my dad is missing somewhere in North Vietnam. He might be dead. My mom is posted to a hospital in Japan. Grandpa is all I've got right now, and if anything happens to him, I've got nobody. What do I do then? Where do I go?"

"Well," she said, 'you've still got me. I'm somebody."

CHAPTER TWENTY-FIVE

Thursday morning at nine o'clock was the time the clerk of the court had set for the hearing for the thirty-seven kids who were caught by the sheriff's deputies at Louise's house party. Between the kids and their parents, Grandpa's courtroom was so crowded that people were spilling out into the hallway. With more people than seats for them to sit in, it was decided to move the hearing downstairs to a community room that was ordinarily used for larger gatherings. A couple of deputies moved quickly to set up rows of folding chairs for those in attendance, plus a table and chair for Grandpa, a second table and chair for the court clerk and the bailiff, and another for the county attorney. It took some time to get all that done, and so the hearing didn't get started until after ten.

As I learned was the usual custom, after everyone was seated, including Mal, Mr. and Mrs. Mueller and me, the bailiff called, "All rise. This court is now in session. The Honorable Judge Harold F. Evans presiding."

Grandpa entered the room from a side door and took his seat. "Everybody just go on ahead and have a seat," he said. "We don't want this to be too formal. We're all neighbors here, and I expect most of us know each other, so let's get comfortable."

I looked at Mal, and I thought we were both probably thinking the same thing, which was, how can anybody get comfortable facing a county judge in a court of law?

Grandpa said, "Before we get started here, let me just cover a few preliminaries. First, nobody here is on trial. This is just a hearing to determine how to proceed. Now in just a minute, I'm going to ask the clerk to read the list of names of those young people who were—what shall we say—who were in attendance at a party at a private home this past Saturday night, just so we're sure everybody who's supposed to be here is here. When you hear your name, I'll ask you to stand and respond by saying 'here' or 'present.' I'll also ask that your parent or whoever is responsible for you to stand up with you and say their name so we know you've got somebody with you. Is that okay with everybody?"

When nobody said anything, Grandpa said, "Mister Clerk, will you go ahead and read the roll?"

The clerk stood and started reading names from a sheet of paper he held in his hand. As Grandpa had asked, as each name was called, a boy or a girl stood up with his or her mother or father and said "here." In a few instances, a parent said something like, "Hey, Judge, is going to take long?" or "Can I just pay the kid's fine and get out of here? I've got work back at the farm," but Grandpa just waved them back down into their seats without taking any notice of their questions.

Some of the names I recognized from the baseball team, including Dennis Smith, Conrad Schmidt and Dave Beatty, the three guys who had missed practice earlier, as well as Louise Porter, the girl at whose house the party took place and also where, as it turned out, a sliding door with a big window had gotten broken. But there were other teammates, including Junior Hanks, whose name, I learned, was actually Arnold, and Craig Blair, one of our utility players. Most of the other names I didn't recognize, although I did remember seeing some of them, boys and girls alike, at Louise's house that night. It did not go unnoticed by everyone who knew us that the clerk did not read my name or the name of Mary Alice Mueller. Dennis, in particular, glared at Mal and me after the clerk finished reading the names. I was sure he figured that somehow Mal and I had skated because of our individual relationships with Grandpa.

"So, now that we've got everybody here, this is how we're going to proceed. Every single person whose name has been read into the record has been charged with misdemeanor trespass, and misdemeanor disorderly conduct and property damage, including breaking a pretty expensive sliding glass door at the Porters' house."

"Now right here I need to tell you that since all of you are juveniles, no matter how you plead, the record of this proceeding will be sealed. That means when you go looking for a job or applying to a college or joining up with the military, you will not be required to admit that you have been arrested, or that you pleaded guilty, if that's what you decide to do, to the charges."

Grandpa paused for a moment before adding, "Does anyone here have any questions about what I've said so far?"

One man in the back raised his hand. Grandpa pointed and said, "Yes, sir? You're Holley Johnson and that's your boy Michael, right?"

"Yes, Judge, it's me, Holley. This here is my son Mike, sure enough."

"Okay, good to see you both. What's your question, Mr. Johnson?"

"Well, I understand about the record being sealed an all, but what I want to know is when I get this rascal home, is it all right if I whup the tar out of him for what he done?"

The courtroom broke out in laughter. Grandpa waited until it died down, and then he said, "Up to you, Mr. Johnson, he's your boy, only I wouldn't be too hard on him. He's still got some growin' up to do. And besides, I seem to remember you being upstairs in this same courthouse answering for one or two of your shenanigans. Or am I thinking about somebody else?"

Mister Johnson found a spot on the floor and stared at it, as if he suddenly found something there to be of great interest. "No, your honor, I guess that was me."

"Thought so," Grandpa said, and again there was laughter. "Anybody else got a question?"

When no one else did, he went on, "All right, then. Well folks, like I said before, this isn't a trial. It's just a hearing. Now if anybody wants to plead not guilty to the charges I've read so far, just see the clerk after we get finished here and we'll go ahead and set a trial date. Otherwise, if you want to plead guilty, just stand up. We'll get everybody's name, then I'll pass sentence and after that most of you can get on home or back to work or whatever else you got to do today. Some of you, though, are going to have to stick around a while longer."

It took a minute and there was the sound of feet shuffling and chairs being pushed back and then every single person in the room, including Mal and her mom and dad stood up. I didn't know what else to do, so I stood up, too.

Grandpa said, "Well, that looks like everybody. Mister and Mrs. Mueller, Mary Alice and Connor, you can sit back down, since this doesn't directly pertain to you."

Mister Mueller said, "Judge, my wife and I talked to Mary Alice about this, and we decided that since she was there at the party, we want to pay our share of the damages."

I said, "I'll pay, too, Grandpa—I mean, Judge Evans. I was there, I'll pay."

Grandpa thought for a moment. "Suit yourselves. The Porters have an estimate for four hundred and eighty-five dollars to repair that sliding door. Pretty expensive door you got there, Mr. Porter, by the way.

"I had to drive all the way to Wellington to get that door, Judge. It was pretty special."

"Well, next time try the lumber yard north of town," Grandpa answered. "I hear they got good prices." And again, the courtroom broke out in laughter.

When things got quieted down, Grandpa continued, "Anyhow, that's about fifteen dollars each for the window, a twenty-dollar fine and twenty-five dollars court costs, so that comes to sixty dollars for each one of you. You can make arrangements to pay at the clerk's office on your way out."

But that wasn't the end of it. Grandpa asked the clerk to read a second list names, this time for the kids who were charged with underage drinking and public intoxication. They and their parents were instructed to remain in the room while the others, about half the original group, were excused.

After that, Grandpa wrapped things up pretty quickly. I thought for sure he was going to come down hard on the kids, and maybe their parents as well, but that's not what happened. First, he threw out the public intoxication charges, since all the drinking took place in the Porters' back yard, which was private property and was strictly speaking, not in public view.

Next, he said that since nobody had been caught driving under the influence, DUI, he called it, he couldn't do anything about revoking or suspending anybody's driver's license. He did ask if anybody wanted to tell him who brought the beer, and to the surprise of no one, no hands went up. I remembered that Kansas was an eighteen state for beer, meaning that almost anybody who looked even close to eighteen could have brought it, and probably more than a few did. I think Grandpa knew that, too, because in the end, all he did was scold the parents still in the room about keeping a closer eye on what their kids were up to, and that if it happened again, he said, there would be serious consequences. Then he nodded to the bailiff who called, "All rise. This court is now adjourned."

Grandpa got up from his seat and walked out of the room, and the people left in the meeting room began filing out. But over the noise of the footsteps, I could hear him in the hallway, coughing again.

CHAPTER TWENTY-SIX

The next morning when I went to the mailbox, I found a letter addressed to me from Laura Westcott, the girl who had kissed me goodbye and asked me to send her my address in Goldenrod. I put Grandpa's mail on the kitchen table and then went back outside to sit on the porch and read what she had written. It said:

Dear Connor,

I was glad to finally get your letter. I was on vacation with my family when it first arrived. This year, my mom and dad decided they wanted to drive up the coast, all the way from Fresno to San Francisco to Portland to Seattle and back. Mostly it was boring, and I was stuck in the back seat the whole way with my stupid sister, who kept needing to stop to go to the bathroom. But there were some spots along the ocean that were really cool, and my dad took some pictures of Mom and Jenny and me standing by the water. The best part was going up to the top of the Space Needle in Seattle. The view from up there is unbelievable. Then, after we got back, it was two more days before my mom finally went to the post office to pick up the mail, so I only just got to read your letter yesterday.

Anyway, it's good to know that you have arrived safely in wherever it is in Kansas that your grandfather lives. I don't think I've ever heard of Goldenrod, but if I can find a Kansas map, I'll try to see if I can find it. I hope you get a chance to make some new friends and that you get to do something besides just sit around the house. Maybe you can find a way to play some baseball. I know you like to do that.

There isn't anything much going on here, but then, I guess you know that since you've been living here for a while. Most days we go to the community pool in the park. I met some older kids there who have their driver's licenses, and at night we go cruising up and down Highway 99 going to drive-ins and meeting other people. I think that's going to get boring after a while because all the boys want to do is race their cars on the highway and try to get us girls to make out with them. No thank you.

You didn't mention in your letter if you heard anything more about your dad. If you did, I hope it's good news and that he has been found and is safe and well. Back here we're all praying for him and for you and your mom.

Well, I guess that's all I have for now. Write and let me know how you are doing.

Your friend,

Laura

Wait a second. Your friend? I read Laura's letter again, and then a third time. Where was the kiss she gave me before I left? Where was the "I'll see you when you get back," or even, "I can't wait for you to get back"?

I was still holding the letter in my hands when Mal and her mother drove up to begin their housekeeping chores.

"Letter from home?' she asked. "Is that from your girlfriend?"

I nodded, yes.

"You don't look happy. Did she break up with you already?"

I shrugged and handed it to her so she could read it for herself.

"Doesn't sound like much of a girlfriend," she said after she finished. "Guess maybe you guys got your wires crossed when you said your good-byes."

"Looks that way."

"Well," she sat down next to me and leaned in close, "that's her loss. And whatever happens between now and when you go back to California, I want you to think about something."

"What is it?"

"Something my dad told me once. He said, there's a very good reason why the windshield in the car is so much bigger than the rear-view mirror."

At that moment, I didn't understand what she was getting at. But later, when I was in bed and having trouble falling asleep, I realized what she meant. And she was right.

CHAPTER TWENTY-SEVEN

On Saturday we finally got back to playing baseball, though not against the team we were scheduled to play the day following the assassination of Robert Kennedy earlier in the month. Instead, we had an away game in Blackwell, Oklahoma, which was just over the state line from Kansas. Grandpa said he wasn't feeling well and asked if I would mind if he didn't come to the game. I was disappointed because Mr. Curtis had said I would be our starting pitcher today, but I kept it to myself and told Grandpa I'd try to win the game for him. He wished me luck and then sat on the porch with me until Robbie and Mr. Curtis came to pick me up. Mister Curtis had borrowed a church bus for the day, so all fifteen of us players would be riding down to Oklahoma together. Before she and her mom finished up at Grandpa's house on Friday, Mal had said she would try to come down, and that she would bring Louise and a couple of her other girlfriends if she could get her mom to let her have the Crapmobile for the day.

As it turned out, the Blackwell Braves, as they were called, was a team made up entirely of American Indians who lived in the area and who attended high school located on a nearby government reservation. Our game was to be played on the high school field, which, to put it kindly, looked more like a sandlot than a high school baseball field. There was no grass on the infield, just dirt which had been raked out earlier in the day. However, on the plus side, the bases were clean and white and the foul lines had fresh chalk. The outfield had grass, and had been mowed recently, but a lot of it had been burned to a yellowish-green by the scorching Oklahoma sun. At that, though, it looked like it would be a decent playing surface.

After warmups, a review of the ground rules and the exchange of lineups, the Braves, wearing white uniforms with red caps and red trim, took the field. As was my custom, I watched their pitcher carefully as he took his warmup tosses. He was tall and thin enough that if his uniform had one more button, it might have been enough extra weight to make him fall over on his face. For all that, though, he had a tricky windup motion and a moving fastball that made a hissing noise as it crossed the plate.

First up was our shortstop, Andy Roselli. He looked at a ball, then a strike and then took a mighty lunge at a pitch below the knees that sent a weak dribbler back to the pitcher. One down. Next, our center fielder Larry Griggs ran the count full before drawing a walk. Right fielder Joe West singled up the middle, parking runners on first and second for cleanup hitter Dennis Smith.

"Now you'll see something," Robbie said. "Denny makes a meal out of pitchers like this guy."

"Good enough," I said. "Nothing better than starting a game with the lead."

But if Dennis had a knife and fork in his back pocket, he was going to have to wait until his next at-bat to use them. He fouled off the first pitch, took two more that were outside and then hit a two-hopper to the shortstop who turned it into an easy double play. Inning over.

Walking out to the mound to start the bottom of the first, I saw Mal drive up in the Crapmobile. She had Louise Porter and a couple of other girls I remembered from the party and, later, from court. Mal and Louise waved to me and took seats in the bleachers as the Braves' leadoff man stepped into the box. Their man was short and muscular, like a smaller version of Dennis Smith. As he took his stance, Robbie called time and walked out to the mound.

He tilted his catcher's mask up. "Make a deal with you, Connor. How about I call the pitches and give you a target and you throw the ball right where I tell you?"

"What?"

"I've seen these guys before. You haven't."

"Fine with me," I said.

"You got a curve?"

"Not that's any good."

"Okay, then. One for heat, two for the curve and three for a change. You got anything else? Slider maybe?"

"Nope, that's about it."

"Then this will be easy," he said, and trotted back behind the plate. I heard him say to the umpire, "New guy. We're just getting our signals straight."

Robbie called the first pitch chest-high and over the inside corner. Swing and a miss. Next, I threw a fastball in the dirt, which their guy started to swing at, but checked in time. One-and-one. Eventually, he worked the count full before lining a shot right into Junior Hanks's mitt at first. So far, so good.

The next hitter, I recognized, was the Braves third baseman. Robbie signaled for the deuce. Knowing my curveball was not very good, I shook him off. He showed me two fingers again, so I gave him what he asked for. The hitter saw it coming and guessed, rightly, there wasn't going to be much of a break. He swung and lined an easy single into center field, which Larry Griggs misjudged. The ball got past him and by the time he got it back into the infield, the runner was standing on third. The next hitter didn't mess around, either, hitting a changeup so hard and so far, it might have bounced all the way back to Kansas after it cleared the left field fence.

Crap. Two to nothing.

After that, I found a rhythm and set the next two hitters down with an infield popup and a grounder to short.

"My fault," Larry said when we got back to the bench. "I booted it."

"Don't worry about it," I told him. "That dinger could have brought a dead man home from the cemetery."

I pitched two more innings, giving up nothing more than a bloop single to right. Meantime, our guys got one run back in the top of the second, thanks to a double by Junior Hanks and a single by Dave Gomez, our second baseman.

It was still 2-1 beginning the bottom of the fourth when Mr. Curtis replaced me with Conrad Schmidt, who would have ordinarily been our starter if he hadn't missed the last practice. The Braves wasted no time lighting him up like a string of firecrackers, and before the inning was over, the score was 7-1. We scored once in the fifth after Dennis Smith struck out on a pitch in the dirt that got past the catcher, allowing Robbie to score from third. Johnny Melendez pitched the sixth and seventh, giving up one more run and then it was over. Braves 8, Copperheads, 2.

After we shook hands with the Braves, Robbie and Mr. Curtis gathered the bats and balls we brought. One of the Braves players, their starting pitcher, waved me over.

"Good game, pitch," he said. "You did all right.

"Connor Ward," I said. "You did all right yourself.

"John Thompson," he said, shaking my hand. He must have seen something in my expression. He laughed and said, "What? Did you think my name was Geronimo?"

Before I could answer, he said, "Maybe you'll get us next time," and walked off.

I went over and sat down on the bleachers next to Mal, Louise and the other two girls who introduced themselves as Robin and Kathleen. "Call her Kate," Robin said.

"You did okay, Connor," Louise said. "Mister Curtis should have let you pitch another inning."

I shook my head. "Conrad is our starter. He had to sit out at the beginning because he missed a practice."

"Well, that's stupid," said Robin. "He's the starter and he should start." It was then that I remembered I had seen Robin with Conrad at

Louise's party. At the same moment, Dennis Smith came over and stood next to where we were sitting.

"Still hanging around with Goldilocks, Mal? Or are you ready to come back with me. I'll even apologize for whatever it is you're mad about if it'll make you feel better."

She threw him a disgusted look. "Get lost."

"Yeah? You know," he said, loud enough for the rest of the team and anybody else within earshot to hear, "it was Mal and Goldilocks who called the cops on us at the party. That's how come they left early, so they could get to a phone and ruin things for everybody else."

"The deputies were already on their way when Mal and Connor left," Louise said, just as loudly. "I called them myself after you idiots broke our window. I wanted you and your drunken friends out of there before the rest of my house got torn down. I just wish they'd charged you with something that would have landed your sorry ass in jail."

The bus ride back to Goldenrod was mostly quiet. A few of the guys were talking in low tones about how the game might have turned out differently if only this or that had happened, instead of what actually did. I sat up near the front, next to Robbie. Dennis was the last to board the bus. He took the seat directly across from Robbie and me and stared at me without saying anything almost the entire way back. It was then that I knew for sure that trouble was coming, and that, when the time came, there would be no getting out of its way.

CHAPTER TWENTY-EIGHT

After the game in Blackwell, the next few weeks went by quickly. The Copperheads played six more games, three in Goldenrod and three on the road in nearby towns. During that stretch, we won four and lost two, giving us a 7-4 record for the season. I pitched in four of the games, getting one win, nailing down two saves and mopping up in a crushing 15-6 loss. In that game, because we trailed by only five runs at the end of the fifth, we had to play all seven innings instead of five, which would have been the case if we had been behind by ten. In the two games I saved, I threw four innings giving up two hits, one walk and no runs. In the big loss, I got tagged for a last-inning home run that brought in the other team's last two runs.

Conrad Schmidt, our starter, seemed to have found a groove and Johnny Melendez pitched well enough in middle relief in our other loss, a 7-6 squeaker. Meanwhile, Robbie and Junior each went on a hitting tear, driving in most of our runs in the wins and at least getting on base in the loss. Dennis Smith, on the other hand, seemed to have disappeared off the end of the earth, getting only three hits during the entire six-game stretch. His average dropped from .625, where it was at the beginning of the season, to around .250 since.

Coach Curtis made sure he got extra batting practice and then dropped him from third to sixth and then seventh in the order, hoping that the change might take some of the pressure off him. Nothing, though, seemed to help, and I thought maybe his slump had to do with the fact that after his day in court, his father took away his car keys for a month. And he'd made it clear to anyone who would listen that he blamed Mal and me for every bit of that, never mind that we had nothing to do with it.

Grandpa was making weekly trips to Wichita to see Dr. Morrow, the oncologist, who had started him on chemo treatments for his cancer. On one of the trips, he took me along, and with Grandpa's permission, I had a chance to talk with the doctor. He was a nice man, not quite Grandpa's age. He had kind eyes and spoke in a quiet voice, looking me in the eye the whole time. I decided I liked him.

"Judge Evans has Stage 2 cancer in his right lung," he told me. "That means the cancer is not only in the lung but in the lymph nodes as well, and that means there's a strong possibility of it spreading to his other organs. Right now, the plan is to treat it with chemotherapy, which is basically a mix of some pretty strong drugs designed to kill the cancer cells. After we administer the treatment, he isn't going to feel very well for a day or two after."

"And that's it?" I asked. "He just has to take some medicine? No radiation?"

Doctor Morrow seemed surprised by the question. "Do you know something about radiation?"

"My mother is a doctor," I explained. She's in Japan, stationed at a military hospital. She mentioned radiation during our last telephone call."

"I see." He paused, as if to gather his thoughts. "Well then, we might get to radiation, but I want to try chemo first, to see if we can keep the cancer from spreading. If we can do that, then we can use radiation to try to force it into remission."

"If that doesn't work, are you going to remove his lung?"

He hesitated for a moment, and I could tell he was being careful about choosing his next words. "If the chemo and the radiation don't give the results we want, then surgery will be the next option. However, that will involve removing part of the lung and the lymph nodes. I just wish we had caught this sooner. I'm betting you understand what that's all about."

I did. The survival rate for cancer patients is directly affected by how early in the disease's progression it's caught. That's why certain cancers are almost always fatal, because the symptoms don't show up until it's too late. I could only hope the doctor caught Grandpa's cancer in time to save his life.

Going home that day, Grandpa said he was tired, and asked me to drive us back to Goldenrod. I did okay, too. I held our speed at a steady 65 miles an hour and stayed in my lane the whole way. Once or twice somebody in a hurry passed me up. I asked if I should speed up, but Grandpa said don't worry about it, we're going the speed limit and for the time being that was fast enough. When we got back, Grandpa went straight to his bedroom and closed the door. I didn't see him again until the next day.

Other evenings, after supper, Grandpa and I kept up my driving lessons, and I had gotten pretty good at wheeling his big car around town and up and down the county highways. A good thing, too, because my birthday was coming up pretty soon. That meant I could get my license, and then I'd probably have to do most of the driving to and from Wichita. Not that I minded. Any opportunity to get behind the wheel of the Cadillac was something to look forward to. I only wished the purpose of the drive could be for something more enjoyable than taking Grandpa for a cancer treatment.

Mom settled into a routine of calling once a week, on Sunday evenings for us, and because of the time difference, Monday mornings for her. After a while, it got to where it seemed like we were following a script, because our conversations never seemed to stray far from the same topics. Mom would ask, how was I doing? Had I made any new friends?

"Yes," I'd tell her, but I didn't bring up my troubles with Dennis Smith, or my closer relationship (more on that later) with Mal. I also didn't tell her that Grandpa had been giving me driving lessons. I wasn't sure how she'd feel about that, and I didn't want her to have to worry about me getting into a head-on collision with an eighteen-wheeler hauling fertilizer on the Kansas Turnpike. I knew from experience with some of my friends back in California, moms tend to worry about stuff like that.

"Yes," I said, answering her next question, I was still playing baseball, and most games I got to pitch at least an inning or two. I even came to bat twice, striking out once and blooping an "excuse me" single to left field the other time. Then it would be my turn, and of course, I'd ask about Dad, and she would tell me that there was no news. But since his body hadn't been recovered, nor had he been on film recorded by the North Vietnamese, who made it a practice of parading their POW's in front of a movie camera, there was still hope he was alive and struggling to find his way back to friendly territory. If I thought talking about Dad would upset her, I was wrong. It wasn't as if she had given up on the idea of ever seeing him again. Instead, she sounded more like she had decided that whatever the outcome was going to be, she was resigned to it. And in any event, until we knew something definite one way or the other, she was determined to keep her emotions under control, at least when she was talking to me.

After all the questions were asked and answered, she'd tell me about her work at the hospital. She wasn't working much with combat casualties, other than to do preliminary examinations when they first came in. She wasn't a surgeon, either, so most of the patients she saw were military men and women with more common complaints and illnesses, although she did administer antivenin to a person who had been bitten by a venomous sea snake. Also, once a week she would fly over to Okinawa, a Japanese island which had become a U. S. territory after World War II, to visit patients at Marine Corps Air Station Futenma. So far, she said, the most interesting thing she had done was deliver triplets for the wife of a Marine gunnery sergeant.

After she finished with me, she'd ask to talk to Grandpa. I tried not to listen in, but I knew she was asking him a lot of questions about his cancer treatments. Those conversations always ran long. I guessed that was because he was trying not to let on how sick he actually was, and she had to keep digging until she could find out what she wanted to know.

Here in Kansas, my relationship with Mal had progressed to the point that it was generally understood among the kids in Goldenrod that we were "going together." Most days Mal accompanied her mom when Mrs. Mueller came to Grandpa's house to take care of the cooking and the cleaning. Mal, of course, was expected to help her mom with the cleaning, and sometimes with other jobs like peeling carrots or potatoes or cutting up apples or peaches to make a pie. Mrs. Mueller's attitude toward me seemed to have warmed up as well. I guess she had gotten over being mad about what happened at Louise's party.

On days when Mal didn't come, or when she expected to be busy helping out all day, I worked in the yard cutting the grass or pulling weeds out of Grandpa's flower beds. Other times, I'd go for a bike ride. But that still left lots of time for us to sit on Grandpa's big front porch and hold hands and talk about whatever was on our minds. The one thing that we did not discuss, not ever, was what was going to happen at the end of the summer when my mother came back from Japan and I would be going home to California.

Over the Fourth of July weekend, Sunflower County held a three-day celebration, with carnival rides, entertainment, arcade games and food tents. There was music from local garage bands and some one-hit-wonder acts like Music Machine and Jeannie C. Riley. Mal and I went to the fair on Saturday and spent the afternoon going on rides, playing arcade games and sampling food, including cotton candy, elephant ears and something called deep-fried pigs' ears—it tasted a little like bacon—that I had never run across back in California. There was a ride called "Zero Gravity," which looked like half of a Ferris wheel that swung back and forth like a pendulum until it finally made a complete rotation. During that part of the ride, it stopped for a minute or at the top of its arc, so that everybody on board was left hanging upside down in their seats. Mal thought it was pretty cool, but it was all I could to keep from throwing up all the food we had been eating.

Once we were back on solid ground, I spotted a shooting gallery where they gave you ten shots with a .22 rifle to try to hit moving objects, like a chain of ducks that moved in a row, and targets that looked like big lollipops swaying back and forth. Thanks to the many hours of practice that I had gotten at the Marine Corps target range at Lemoore, hitting the targets was not difficult at all.

On my first try, I got all ten and won a black-and-white stuffed panda, which I gave to Mal. She promised she would keep him forever. She even decided she would name him Connor.

Toward evening, the air got a little cooler and the loud music that had been blaring over the loudspeaker system was turned off. Some people drifted over to a main stage to listen to speeches from the chairman of the Sunflower County Board of Supervisors, and a congressman named Robert Dole, who was running for the United States Senate in the fall. He gave a talk that was supposed to be about patriotism, but to me sounded more like a campaign speech. Grandpa, in his role as county judge was even asked to get up and say a few words. His speech turned out to be very few words, indeed, as he started coughing after a few minutes and had to make his apologies. I asked whether he wanted me to drive him home, but he said no, he'd be fine. And besides, he said, we hadn't done much practicing driving at night.

By the time Grandpa took off for home, it was getting dark, so Mal and I wandered over to the main grandstand where the fireworks show was to take place. We had just gotten settled into our seats when the lights all around the celebration site went dark and a recording of the National Anthem was played over the loudspeakers. Then the fireworks show, which lasted almost an hour, began. It was a pretty good show, and it was nearly ten o'clock when the last of the skyrockets lit up the sky in a big finish. Then the carnival lights came back up, and there was an announcement that closing time would be at eleven o'clock, which gave everyone another hour to enjoy a few more rides or arcade games or maybe wolf down another deep-fried pig's ear.

I asked Mal what she wanted to do and she said she thought it was time to go. She wanted to get ahead of the traffic, and besides, she said, there was something she wanted to show me on the way back. And so, Mal and I headed for home. But not before she drove us to the spot she had wanted to take me the night we went to Louise's party.

CHAPTER TWENTY-NINE

The Wednesday after the Fourth of July celebration I got a telephone call from Robbie Curtis. "Connor, how would you like to go crow hunting with Junior and me?"

"I never heard of that," I said. "Why would anybody hunt for crows? Do you eat them?"

"Nobody eats them. They're nothing but varmints. You just shoot them and let them lay. Other crows see 'em and fly in to take a look. Pretty soon, you got a whole pile of crows you can leave for the raccoons and the coyotes to eat later on."

I wanted to say that was the dumbest thing I ever heard, but then I thought, well, if I really wanted to fit in, crow hunting might be as good a way as any to do it.

"Okay," I told Robbie. "When?"

"Pick you up around two o'clock if that's okay."

"Just one thing," I said, "I don't have a gun."

"Don't worry about it. I'll bring you one."

"You're doing what?" Mal said when I told her.

"Crow hunting. With Robbie and Junior. Robbie said his dad has lots of guns. He's going to bring one I can borrow."

"Well," she said, "don't bring 'em back here."

"The crows or the guns?"

"Neither one."

Robbie and Junior showed up at Grandpa's house a little after two. Junior was driving, since Robbie was still forbidden to drive except to and from work. Junior's ride was a battered Chevrolet pickup with a gun rack that held three long guns in the rear window. Mal came out on the porch to watch as we headed out on our hunting trip.

"Hey, Mal," Robbie called out. "Want us to bring you back some crow feathers?"

"You know what you can do with 'em," she called back. "You boneheads try not to shoot one another."

Robbie opened the door on the passenger side and got out. "You get the middle seat, Connor. I got the window."

The window was a good choice. The middle seat was not. Junior's truck had very little ventilation other than the open windows, and the outside temperature was close to a hundred degrees, making it uncomfortably hot in the middle. It was a clear day, dry and dusty, with no breeze and the sun hammering down on the Kansas farm country the way it does in the California desert. I hoped that, wherever we were going, there would at least be some shade.

"So, tell me how this works," I said. "Do we have to chase after the crows or do they come to us?"

"Naw," Junior said, "we got a plastic owl and some crow decoys in the back. We just set 'em all out and the crows will come after the owl, 'specially when they see the crow decoys."

"Crows hate owls," Robbie added. "The love to torment 'em. We're going out to a field of winter wheat where the farmer has already made his first cut. There'll be lots of loose grain on the ground. When the crows come for the grain, they'll see the owl and take after him. Then we just pop 'em and leave 'em lay. From a distance, it'll attract more crows to the owl."

"More crows, more targets," Junior said. "You ever shoot a shotgun? You need a lesson?"

"My father is a Navy officer," I said. "Sometimes I go with him to the practice range on the base. I've shot everything from a sniper rifle to an M16 on full rock and roll. I think I can figure this out."

"That's cool," Junior said, and I could tell he was impressed.

Robbie spotted a small opening in a tree line alongside the field where he and Junior had planned our hunt. Junior handed me one of the three shotguns they had brought along and, while I inspected it to make sure it was unloaded, as is standard military procedure, he and Junior placed the plastic owl about fifteen yards from where we had taken cover. Then they spotted three crow decoys around the owl to make it look like the crows were getting set to attack.

"Now, what?" I said when they returned and concealed themselves in the bushes.

"Now what we do is call 'em in." Junior reached into his overalls pocket and pulled out a crow call, which looked like a short, fat wooden tube with a metal mouthpiece at one end. When he blew on the mouthpiece, it made a "Kaw-Kaw" squawking noise that actually did sound something like the noise a crow makes. I found this both interesting and funny, and while Robbie and Junior hid themselves in the bushes, I climbed up on a fallen log in a clear area just behind us where I could watch and see what would happen next. Besides, I thought, I was happy just to be spending part of the day with a couple of new friends. If I didn't actually shoot any crows, that would be okay, too. Anyway, it didn't seem quite right to shoot and kill something just for the sake of killing it.

In fact, as it turned out, nobody killed anything, or even fired a shot that day. No matter how hard Junior blew on his crow-caller, no birds appeared in the sky. After fifteen or twenty minutes, he stopped to catch his breath.

And then he started scratching. And so did Robbie.

"I'm starting to itch all over," Junior said. "What the hell? Are we sitting on an ant hill or something?"

"Don't think so," Robbie said, and they both started looking around.

It wasn't an ant hill, though. It was poison ivy, a vine that produces leaves in clusters of three. The oil on the leaves causes intense itching and raises watery blisters when it comes in contact with human skin. Worse, the itching and the blisters can last for several days or more, and no amount of anti-itching cream or lotion seems able to provide much relief.

Mal laughed when Junior dropped me back at Grandpa's house and I told her how our day had gone.

"And you didn't shoot any crows," she said, laughing like it was the funniest story she'd ever heard.

"You didn't sit next to them on the way back, did you?"

"I sat in the back of the truck."

"Good thing. I told you those two were a

couple of boneheads. You're lucky you didn't get into that stuff yourself. But just to make sure, go inside and take the hottest shower you can stand. And next time," she said, grabbing me by the collar of my shirt and kissing me, "listen to me when I tell you something is a bad idea."

Robbie and Junior had showed up for baseball practice on Tuesday, so they both were eligible to start Thursday night's game. However, on game night, whether they were on the bench between innings or in the field, they seemed to be spending nearly all their time scratching, much to the amusement of both teams. In the top of the second, Junior let a ground ball go through his legs and Robbie let two Conrad Schmidt fastballs in the dirt skip all the way to the backstop. He was actually scratching while he chased the ball.

By that time, Coach Curtis had seen enough. He sent Dave Simon in to replace Robbie behind the plate and me to first base to play for Junior. It didn't really make any difference that two of our strongest hitters spent the rest of the game sitting and scratching. The team we were playing wasn't very good, and by the fifth inning the Copperheads were ahead 15-2, so the game was called on account of the mercy rule after the fifth. I even got a hit and drove in a couple of runs. Better still, Grandpa was at the game to see me do it. But the best news of all is that our record improved to eight wins, four losses. If we could win one of our remaining two games, we would qualify for a regional tournament that could take us to Wichita for the final round.

CHAPTER THIRTY

That night after supper, Grandpa asked me if I'd be willing to drive up to Wichita with him in the morning. "Doctor's going to give me another chemo treatment," he said. "This is getting to be hard on me, and I might not be feeling well enough to drive back. You don't mind riding along, do you? Get you some practice driving on the highway coming back."

"Okay, Grandpa," I said. "I don't mind coming along."

"I'll call Loretta Mueller and tell her to take the day off, since we might not be back for supper. I'm probably not going to be hungry, because that treatment really upsets my stomach. So, we can stop and pick something up for you on the way back. That be all right with you?"

"That will be fine." Then I said, "Grandpa, how about if I call Mal—Mary Alice—and tell her she and her mom can stay home tomorrow. There's something I want to talk to her about, anyway."

"Go ahead," he said, and went into the living room to turn on the television.

I dialed the number for the Mueller residence. Mal's father picked up on the second ring.

"Mister Mueller?" I began.

"This is Doctor Mueller."

Doctor Mueller, right. Crap, I forgot! He's a veterinarian.

"Sorry," I said. "Doctor Mueller, this is Connor Ward. I'm staying with my grandfather, Judge Evans."

"Oh, yes, Connor, of course. How are you getting along here in the middle of nowhere?"

"Just fine, sir. I am getting a little homesick, though."

"Understandable. And how is your grandfather? I understand he's got a bit of a health concern."

"He'll be okay, I think. He's a fighter, and he's pretty tough."

"I hope so, Connor. And you know, everybody in town is rooting for him."

"Thank you." I couldn't think of anything else to say.

There was a pause. "But I'm guessing you didn't call to talk to me."

"Actually, I was calling for Mrs. Mueller. Grandpa has to go to Wichita for . . . on a business trip. He wanted me to tell Mrs. Mueller she could take the day off tomorrow because we might be home late."

"I understand," he said. "I'll let my wife

know. By the way, Connor, Mary Alice is standing right here. I think she wants to talk to you because she looks like she's about to jump out of her skin."

In the background I heard Mal say, "*Daddy-y-y!*" Then to me she said, "Hey Connor, what's up?"

"Nothing really. Grandpa asked me to call and let your mom know we're going to Wichita tomorrow to see the doctor. Grandpa doesn't really like to eat after his treatment, so you and your mom might as well take the day off."

"Oh," she said, sounding disappointed. "I thought maybe you wanted to talk to me."

"Actually, I do, if you've got a minute." But she must have heard something in my voice, because before I could tell her what it was, she said, "I'm coming over. I don't think this is something I want you to tell me over the phone."

In fact, I had been mentally rehearsing what I wanted to tell Mal for a couple of days, since the night of the Fourth of July celebration, when it took us a lot longer to get home than it would have if we had come straight back. The thing was, I liked her a lot, and I knew she liked me. But July was nearly over and then we would be into August and not long after that I would be on my way back to California. That left me with the choice of either starting to back away from her now, or let things go on as they were until it was time to go home, when our separation would be that much harder. Plus, I'd be getting my driver's license in a couple of weeks and Grandpa didn't seem to be getting any better. In all likelihood, I'd be spending more of the time I still had in Goldenrod driving him back and forth to Wichita, which meant I'd have even less time for Mal.

I didn't know a good way to explain all this to her, or that she'd understand when I did. But either way, I only had about ten minutes to come up with something.

"Wait, you're breaking up with me?"

"No. Not breaking up, just, I don't know, stepping back a little."

Mal must have set some kind of land speed record over the distance between her house and Grandpa's. It seemed as though I had barely hung up the phone when the Crapmobile skidded to a stop in our driveway. I was sitting out on the front porch steps, waiting. I thought it might not be a good idea to have this discussion in the house. I knew Grandpa wasn't one to eavesdrop, but I also knew if voices were raised, he wouldn't be able to help but overhear and I didn't want to bother him with my problems.

"You got another letter from that girl back in California, didn't you? What's her name, Laura?"

"Yes. No. Yes. I mean yes, her name is Laura, and no, I didn't get any letters except the one you saw right after I got here. I don't think she's interested in me."

"Then what?"

"I just think—Mal, I'm only going to be here another month or so, and then I have to go back to California. I may never see you again after that. For all I know, I could end up in Japan with my mom if the Navy orders her to stay there past the end of August. I'm not breaking up with you. I'm just saying it might be a good idea if we pulled back a little. Because if we keep going like we are, the way we did on the way home from the celebration . . . well, you know."

"You mean because I let you put your hands on me? You're worried we're going to go all the way?" And then her eyes began to tear up as an idea came to her.

"Or is that what you want? Is that what this is about? Give you what you want or we're through?"

"No, Mal, no. It's not like that at all. When I found out I was coming to Goldenrod, leaving California was just about the last thing in the world I wanted to do. I wanted to be home with my mom so that we'd be there when my dad came home from wherever he is right now. I wanted to be with my friends, and yes, I thought that might include Laura Westcott.

"But it hasn't worked out that way, and the only good thing that's happened to me since I've been here is you. And if we keep going like we are, when I do have to leave, it's going to be that much harder for both of us. I get it that you've just come off a bad breakup, and I don't want to be just another bad memory for you."

She sat quietly for a few moments. "Connor, let me ask you something. If you knew for sure, and I mean without any question at all, that the world was going to come to an end tomorrow, would you spend today hiding under your bed? Or do you think maybe you'd walk outside into the sunshine and breathe the air for as long as you could?"

"I see what you're saying," I said. "I was just trying to make things easier."

"Saying goodbye to someone you care for is never easy, Connor, so let me tell you a story. One that I think you'll like."

"Okay." But I couldn't imagine any story she could tell me that would make me feel better.

"It goes like this. The next time your mom calls, she's going to tell you that your dad has turned up safe, and that he wasn't taken prisoner, but that he got hurt when he bailed out of his plane and he's going to be in the hospital for a while.

Your mom is going to arrange for you to get a military flight to Japan where you'll all be together for a couple of weeks and then you're going to come back to Goldenrod because you dad can't travel and you mom is going to stay with him. Meantime, your grandfather is going to get well and you're going to live in his house for at least the next school year."

"And what if none of that ever happens? Or even if it does, what then?" I asked.

"Then, I'll have another story for you. One that you'll like even more."

CHAPTER THIRTY-ONE

The next morning, Grandpa and I were up and out early. We had an hour drive to Wichita and he had an early appointment with his doctor, only this time it was at a clinic and not at the doctor's office. Grandpa checked in at a reception desk in the lobby. The person behind the counter handed him a clipboard that held several forms and a pen to fill them out. When he finished, the receptionist snapped a plastic bracelet on his wrist and then told him someone would come get him and take him to the treatment area. She said I could go up in the elevator with him if it was okay with Grandpa.

"The boy goes where I go," he told her.

After a few minutes an attendant dressed in a white shirt and white pants arrived, pushing a wheelchair. Grandpa said he could walk, but the attendant said, "House rules. I do the driving. You get to take a ride."

Grandpa sat in the wheelchair and the three of us went down the hall to an elevator. The attendant pushed a button and we rode up two floors. When the doors opened, we were in a large waiting area that looked like a hotel lobby, with recliner chairs and tables stacked with newspapers and magazines. There was a television in the corner with the sound turned down low, so that only people sitting near it could hear.

A nurse took the clipboard with the papers Grandpa had filled out. She asked him a few questions about how he was feeling, was he sleeping okay, was he able to keep his meals down and whether he was having any other problems. When he said no, she said "Okay, then," took the clipboard and disappeared into a back room. When she came back, she had an IV stand with a bag of clear liquid hanging from it. She had Grandpa move into one of the recliner chairs and asked him to take off his suit jacket and roll up his left sleeve. Then she tied a tourniquet around his arm just above the elbow.

"Little stick," she said, and inserted an IV needle into a vein on the back of Grandpa's hand and taped it into place so it wouldn't back out if he moved his arm. Then she attached the IV tube to the needle and removed the tourniquet. She adjusted a valve on the IV bag and fluid began flowing down the tube and into Grandpa's arm.

I had to hand it to him. The whole time this was going on, he didn't complain, didn't flinch, didn't ask any questions.

The nurse gave him a little bell with a handle on one end. "If you have any problems or start to feel sick, or if you need to use the washroom, just ring. I'll come back a couple times to make sure you're doing okay. Otherwise, just relax. This will take about an hour, and then we'll get you back home, okay?"

I said, "Can I ask what chemical we're using here?"

Her eyebrows went up. "Are you in medical school?"

"My mother is a doctor. She's in the Navy, stationed in Japan. When she calls, I'm pretty sure she'll ask."

"And is this your grandfather?"

I nodded, "Yes."

The nurse smiled. "Well, then, I'll write it down for you so you don't have to try to remember it. We're using an alkylating agent that makes it hard for cancer cells to reproduce. Your mom will recognize what it is."

Sometimes it doesn't pay to be a doctor's kid. I knew from reading some of Mom's books that cancer is a disease where abnormal cells in the body begin to reproduce out of control and eventually crowd out normal cells, so that the affected organs can't work right. Worse, these abnormal, or malignant, cells sometimes move from one organ to another, through a process called metastasis, and spread the cancer to other areas of the body. Once this happens, treatment becomes more complicated and a cure becomes more difficult. The best outcomes occur, as any doctor will tell you, when the disease is caught early. I hoped that was true in Grandpa's case, but I knew coughing up blood was not a hopeful sign.

I also knew there were going to be side effects. Because the chemicals used in therapy can't tell good cells from bad ones, they also attack healthy cells, resulting in hair loss, a weakened immune system, mouth sores, difficulty breathing, vomiting and diarrhea. No matter how things turned out in the end, Grandpa was in for a very rough ride

After the nurse left, I said, "Grandpa, are you doing okay? You don't look so good."

"I'm okay. I'm just tired, and this medicine makes me feel a little out of sorts."

"Can I bring you anything? Some coffee, or some water?"

He shook his head. "Don't think I could keep it down. Listen, I have to ask you. Has Mary Alice talked to you about the dance at the country club?"

"Wait a minute, what? There's a dance? At a country club?"

"Well, it's not really a country club. I mean it looks more like a cow pasture than a golf course, and anybody can pay a couple hundred bucks and get a season pass. But they do have a dance every year for all the high school kids, right before it's time to head back to school. I expect she'll be wanting you to take her."

My mind skipped back to the conversation I'd had with Mal the day before. "She hasn't said anything about it."

"That's probably because she's waiting for you to ask her."

"How do you know that?"

"Her mother told me. Make sure you don't let any grass grow on it when we get back. You don't want her to have to say no to somebody else while she's waiting for you."

Oh, man. This is exactly what I was trying to avoid when I suggested to Mal that maybe we should slow things down. Grandpa wasn't sure of the date, but it seemed likely that the dance would take place very close to the time I would be packing up to go back to Fresno. That figured to be a very emotional time for both of us and closing things out with what sounded like a pretty special event was going to make things even harder.

"I don't know, Grandpa," I said. "Maybe it would be better if she did go with somebody else. I mean, I'm not going to be around that much longer, and I think she's beginning to get attached to me."

"And you don't care about her, is that what you're saying? Listen, Connor, I don't know much about how kids go about falling in love these days, if that's what you're doing, or if you're just hanging on to each other for some other reason.

"But if I didn't know it before, this cancer is teaching me that you have to live in the moment, because none of us knows what tomorrow is going to look like. Sometimes things have a way of working themselves out in ways we never expect, so why not just keep on doing what you're doing, take Mary Alice to the dance and see what happens?"

Grandpa seemed to perk up a little on the drive back to Goldenrod, so much so that he suggested we stop along the way and have lunch. That was for my benefit, though, because when the food came, he decided he wasn't very hungry after all, and just picked at what was on his plate. I was disappointed, but not surprised. I knew that loss of appetite resulting from nausea is one of the side effects of chemo, but it did worry me about what would happen if his weight started to drop too much, because he needed to eat in order to keep up his strength.

"Grandpa," I asked when we got back to the car, "do you still miss Grandma?"

"Every day," he said, his voice softening. "We were together more than thirty years, and she was just about everything in the world to me. There's still mornings when I come downstairs in the morning and expect to find her there in the kitchen waiting for me so we can have our coffee together."

"Do you think, after we die, that we're reunited with the people we love while we're here on earth, or do you think those are just words?"

"There's a whole bunch of folks like to believe that" he said. "Me, I just don't know, but I guess I'd like to think so. Time a person gets to be my age, there's a lot of people gone before that you miss. It'd be nice to get a chance to see them again."

When we got back to Goldenrod, Mal and Mrs. Mueller were already at the house, tending to their housekeeping chores. Grandpa said hello and then went straight to his bedroom, he said, for a nap. I told him I'd wake him when it was time for supper, and then I went to find Mal to ask her if she wanted to go with me to the dance.

CHAPTER THIRTY-TWO

On Thursday night we played out next-to-the-last regular season baseball game, against the Blackwell Braves, whose field we had visited earlier and who were now the visiting team at our park. We had a pretty good crowd, as the Braves were undefeated and trying to stay that way. Meanwhile, the Copperheads needed to win one of our last two games to qualify for the regional tournament. In other words, this game meant something, and rooters for both teams turned out to see how things would turn out. The boy scouts had set up a stand selling popcorn, hotdogs and lemonade, and they figured to have a big night raising money for their annual trip to Philmont Ranch in New Mexico. Even better, Robbie and Dave had recovered from their poison ivy-induced itching and scratching, so we were at full strength. Conrad Schmidt was set to go on the mound, and even Dennis Smith seemed to be breaking out of his season-long slump, although Mr. Curtis still had him slotted in the seventh spot in the batting order.

Unfortunately for the Copperheads, the excitement in the home team bleachers did not last beyond the first inning. The Braves' leadoff hitter lined Conrad's first pitch into left field that Dennis Smith misplayed into a two-base error, and just like that there was a man perched on third base before all the fans had even gotten settled in their seats. After that, it got worse. Conrad was plainly upset over Dennis's shaky outfield play and walked the next two batters on nine pitches. Then, with the bases loaded, their cleanup man homered to left-center, and all of a sudden it was 4-0 and we still hadn't gotten anybody out.

Conrad settled down after that and got out of the first without any further damage, but when the Copperheads went down in order in the bottom of the first, it was like the energy had evaporated out of our half of the crowd. As if that wasn't bad enough, the Braves got two more in the second. Mr. Curtis decided Conrad didn't have his best stuff and replaced him with Johnny Melendez to start the third.

Johnny did a little better, holding the Braves scoreless in the third and giving up one run in the fourth. Meanwhile, our hitters couldn't have done worse if they had gone to the plate holding their bats backwards. Robbie managed a single off the Braves' lefty in the second with two out but was stranded when Dennis went down swinging on three pitches. He fanned a second time in the bottom of the fifth, and in frustration, threw his helmet on the ground and kicked it toward our bench. Mr. Curtis immediately sat him down and sent Dave Clyde, a good-field, no-hit outfielder in to replace him in the top of the sixth. When our guys took the field, Dennis walked down to the end of the bench and sat down next to me.

"This is all your fault, you know."

I turned to look at him. The anger that had boiled over a moment ago seemed to have drained out of him altogether. His wide shoulders sagged, and there was something like sadness in his voice.

I said, "You mean it's my fault that we're behind seven-nothing to a better team, or that you can't hit left-handed pitching?"

"I mean, before you got here, everything was good. Now my life sucks."

I started to ask him how that was my fault, but the unmistakable sound of a bat hitting a ball hard caused us both to look toward the field where a Braves hitter had just launched a Johnny Melendez mistake pitch far over the right field fence. As their man trotted around the bases, the Braves side of the stands erupted in cheers, while our fans sat in dejected silence. They had come expecting a good game and hoping for a win, but what they got was a sorry exhibition of Copperhead play at its absolute worst.

"Let me understand this," I said, with some irritation. "The day I got here, I threw you six or seven pitches that you couldn't do anything with.

Are you telling me that every time you face a pitcher you've never seen before you light him up on your first at-bat? Because that's what this sounds like. And if that is your problem, in another month baseball will be over and I'll be back in California. Then you can be a hero again. Go out for football. Or maybe the track team. Do whatever you want, I don't give a shit. Of course, I can't do anything about you and the cops. You did that to yourself."

"Easy for you to say. They didn't bust you."

"That's because I wasn't there. It was just timing. I don't drive. Mal wanted to leave, so we left. She was my ride."

"I'll bet you liked that."

"Okay, I get it," I said. "But the way I heard it, she ditched you because you knocked her around, and not just once, and if that's true, you don't deserve her, and somebody should have kicked your ass."

That must have struck a nerve, because I saw the muscles in his neck and shoulders start to tighten up, and I realized that I might have said more than I should have. I didn't want to get into a fistfight in the middle of a ball game. Not that I was afraid of him by any means. I had spent my entire life around Navy bases where there were lots of Marines who were friends with my mom and dad and who were more than happy to teach me some self-defense tricks. Even though he had about thirty pounds on me, unless Dennis had a weapon or some similar kind of training, as long as he didn't get me down on the ground and use his weight advantage to pin me, I was pretty sure I could take care of myself.

I said, "This is starting to get away from us, so how about this? I'm going to sit at the other end of the bench. You don't talk to me and I don't talk to you, unless it's got something to do with the game. That sound okay to you?"

He didn't seem to hear. "You're taking Mal to the dance?"

"I see her and her mother almost every day, Dennis. I asked her. She said yes."

He got up from his seat and started to walk away, but not before turning to face me. "Unless you're leaving tomorrow and I don't get the chance, I'm gonna crack you open like a walnut, Connor Ward. You're going to be heading home in a body cast."

The Braves got two more runs off Johnny Melendez, and we got three back in the last of the sixth on, of all things, a bases-loaded triple by Dave Clyde. Coach Curtis sent me in to finish up, which I did, striking out one, walking one and then getting the last man I faced on a liner to Junior Hanks for an unassisted double play. We went down quietly in the bottom of the seventh and then it was over. We had one more game to play, on Saturday. If we lost that one, the season was over as well. And the more I thought about it, that would have been fine with me.

CHAPTER THIRTY-THREE

Friday afternoon, a strong wind kicked up out of the southeast and dark clouds began to gather. By Saturday morning, rain was coming down hard, with the promise of more showers off and on for the rest of the weekend. Mister Curtis called about ten-thirty to let me know that our final baseball game of the regular season was postponed until Tuesday night. That left me with nothing to do for the rest of the day, and since Mal and her mother didn't come to Grandpa's house on the weekends, nobody to do it with.

Saturday mornings there wasn't anything on television except cartoons for little kids, so I made some toast with peanut butter and went outside on the porch to watch the rain come down. After a while, Grandpa came out and sat down next to me.

"You look troubled, boy. Something bothering you?"

"No, Grandpa, I'm okay. It's just the game got rained out. I was hoping we'd get this season over today."

"This hasn't been a very good visit for you, has it?"

"It's been okay," I said. "It's just . . .."

"You mean you're okay with being here, you're just not okay with the reason why."

"I don't know. I guess so. I mean, I'm happy to see you. I just wish we were all together, you and me and Mom and Dad. And I wish you didn't—I wish you were feeling better."

"Well, we're doing what we can about that. And I'm grateful you're here to help with the driving. You know, after your mom and your Uncle Jonathan moved away and then Paul and your grandmother died, I was feeling pretty bad myself, and I even took to drinking for a while. But then it came to me one day after I had to sentence a man found guilty of murder that life is a gift, and we might just as well make the most of it every day, because we only get one time around the track."

"That's what Mal said the other day."

He gave me a small smile. "Mary Alice is a smart girl, Connor. She wants to be a veterinarian like her dad. I'm glad the two of you crossed paths and connected the way you did."

"Connected, yeah, I guess maybe we are. But it's just going to be another good-bye for me when I go back to California."

"I thought you were looking forward to going back home."

"Yeah, but back home to where? For now, home is Fresno, but next month it could be Tokyo or Portsmouth or wherever the Navy decides to send us next. I'd just like to go someplace and know we're going to be there long enough to make some real friends. You know, friends that last longer than a year or two."

"No friends here in Kansas, then?"

"I don't know. Robbie and Junior, maybe, and Mal, of course. But I haven't really tried, because about the time I get to know somebody here, I'll be heading home again." I sighed. "I do have somebody that wants to beat me up, though, so no real friends, but one real enemy."

Grandpa gave me a hard look. "Who wants to beat you up?"

"It doesn't matter, Grandpa. I can handle myself."

"It's that Smith kid, isn't it? The one who couldn't hit you if he had a banjo for a bat."

"That's the one, but it's all right. He's just upset with how things are going for him right now. He's in a slump at the plate. He got busted at Louise's party for underage drinking and Mal broke up with him right before I got here. It doesn't have anything to do with me, but he needs somebody to be mad at."

"Well, you need to be careful around him. Dennis Smith has had his problems, and he's been in my courtroom more than just that one time. First time was a few years back when he stole another kid's bicycle. Then there was a fight or two at the school and a couple curfew violations. His mother died about a year ago, and since then his dad's had trouble holding on to a job. Way I hear it, he and his dad and his brother and sister have had to stay with relatives now and again when they're not able to make their rent. I suppose for all that, he's not a bad kid, though. He just needs to do some growing up."

"Grandpa, I'm confused. How come with all the bad things some people do, other people still say, 'he's not a bad guy'?

"That's a good question, Connor. I expect it's because someplace down deep, we all hope they really are good people, because that way we don't have to think about what we're going to do with them when it turns out they aren't."

CHAPTER THIRTY-FOUR

The next week flew almost before I noticed. On Sunday, Mom called, as she always did. I didn't have much of anything new to tell her about. She asked about our baseball team, and I told her we had taken a rainout on Saturday with a makeup game Tuesday. That game would determine whether our season was over, or if we would advance to the first round of a regional playoff.

"That sounds exciting," she said. "What do you think of your chances?"

"Probably pretty good," I told her. "We played these guys earlier in the season and beat them without any trouble, but that was a home game for us. This game is at Winfield, which is about twenty miles from here."

"I know Winfield," she said. "When I was in high school, I dated a boy from Winfield for a couple of months before I met your father."

Then I told her about Grandpa's trips to the cancer center in Wichita, and also the name of the drug he was being given.

"That's some pretty wicked stuff. How is he handling it?"

"It makes him sick to his stomach. He takes me along so I can drive us back to Goldenrod because he doesn't feel well enough to drive himself."

There was a pause on the line that lasted a bit longer than the usual lapse required for the satellite to bounce our conversation back and forth. I could almost hear the gears grinding at her end, and I knew what she was going to say next.

"How is it that you're driving his car?"

"He's been giving me lessons. I've actually gotten pretty good." I let it go at that, though, and I didn't tell her about Grandpa's plan to have me get a Kansas driver's license. I also didn't mention that there was a dance coming up, and that I would almost certainly be picking up Mal in Grandpa's Cadillac.

"Well," she said finally, "I guess if he needs you, then go ahead. Just try not to kill the both of you in the process. Now let me talk to your grandfather."

After I hung up the extension, I remembered that Mal had made a prediction about what Mom would tell me the next time she called. But if she had any good news about Dad, she didn't tell me. And I didn't want to pester her by asking.

Tuesday morning, I went with Grandpa back to Wichita for another round of chemo. As it happened after each of his earlier visits to the cancer treatment, he felt weak and sick to his stomach, meaning that it was up to me to get us back to Goldenrod. Of course, I enjoyed driving Grandpa's car, I just wished our outings together were for something other than doctor visits. We were about halfway back, when Grandpa suddenly started coughing and asked me to stop the car. I pulled over on the side of the road, just in time for him to open the door, lean out and vomit.

I said, "Grandpa?"

"It's okay. Just give me a minute." I waited while he threw up again. Then he retrieved some tissue from the glove compartment and wiped his face. He looked so pale, I thought he might die at any moment. But then he seemed to pull himself together.

"There's a gas station up ahead at the crossroads. Pull in so I can use the washroom and get some water to rinse my mouth out. We'll fill up the car and you can get yourself a soda, or something to eat if you want."

"You should eat something, too, Grandpa."

"Not hungry," he said.

"I know. I know what that medicine does. But just the same, eat a candy bar or a doughnut or something. Mom says you need calories." And so, he bought a sweet roll. And he ate about half of it and threw the rest out the window.

Tuesday night, we all met at our field at four o'clock for a short team meeting before we got on our rattletrap church bus for the forty-five-minute drive to Winfield. It was a hot evening, about what you'd expect for the last week in July in far southern Kansas. For most of the day the temperature had hovered near a hundred degrees, and it hadn't gotten much cooler as game time approached. Both teams took a shorter than usual warmup, and then the game started.

It went pretty much the way I told Mom I thought it would. Our shortstop, Andy Roselli, lined the second pitch he saw for a double down the right field line. Right fielder Joe West followed with a single, and, after two were out, Robbie lifted a high fly ball to center, which the Winfield center fielder lost in the setting sun and just like that it was 3-0.

Mister Curtis had told me before the game that if Conrad ran out of gas, he'd put me in ahead of Johnny Melendez, who was complaining that his knee was sore. It didn't matter, though. Conrad pitched like a man in a dream, setting down one Winfield Warrior after another like they were ten-year-olds

We added runs in the third, fourth and sixth innings, as everybody in the lineup, including Robbie and Dennis got at least one hit and we won going away, 9-2, with Conrad pitching a five-hit, six-inning effort. I closed it out with a three-up, three-down seventh. Mal drove over with Louise and Robin to watch the game, and after we got back to Goldenrod, a bunch of us went to the Dairy Queen to celebrate.

Dennis did not come with us.

CHAPTER THIRTY-FIVE

Following our final regular-season game over Winfield, there was a one-week gap while the rest of the teams in our league finished their seasons, either because of a rainout they had to make up or because their home fields were temporarily unavailable due to other outdoor events like tractor pulls or district fairs. That meant that, before we took the field again against whoever would be our playoff opponent, my sixteenth birthday will have come and gone, and, unless I bombed the test, I'd have my driver's license.

My actual birthday, August second, was on a Friday, but I was going to have to wait until the following Monday to take my driving test, because Tuesdays and Fridays were the days Grandpa had his regular appointment in Wichita for his cancer treatment. For a change, Grandpa let me drive both ways. On the way up, he paged through the handbook for new drivers and quizzed me on the practice questions. They were all pretty simple if you had bothered to read the handbook ahead of time, which I had, three times.

"Okay," he said, flipping to the sample questions in the back of the book, "when passing another vehicle, when it is lawful to exceed the speed limit? When is it safe to pass a school bus that has stopped? Even if you don't see a train, if you see flashing lights when approaching a railroad crossing, you should do what?" (Answers: Never; Only if there are no flashing lights or no stop sign extended; Stop and check both directions before proceeding.)

As it usually did, Grandpa's treatment took a little more than an hour, and then the technician handed him an appointment slip to go to the hospital on Tuesday rather than come to the clinic because Dr. Morrow had ordered some tests to determine whether the chemo was having the desired effect.

Mal and Mrs. Mueller were waiting at the house when Grandpa and I got back from Wichita. To my surprise, Mrs. Mueller had made me a birthday cake, white with chocolate frosting, and she had somewhere found a little plastic model car to put on the top. Grandpa even perked up a little and sat with Mal, Mrs. Mueller and me to have a slice of cake and to sing "Happy Birthday," which embarrassed me a little. Then Mal handed me a package wrapped in birthday paper.

"Go ahead and open it," she said. "I hope it's something you'll like."

"I got you something, too," Grandpa said. "But open the one from Mary Alice first."

Mal's gift turned out to be a copy of the

Baseball Encyclopedia, a 3,000-page book about the size of a telephone directory containing statistics for every major league team, including season results, batting averages, ERA's and world series results, going back to the early 1900s. If there were ever a player or a team you wanted to find out something about, this was the book to have.

"Wow," I said, flipping through the pages.

"I might never put this down."

Grandpa's gift was a black Wichita State University sweatshirt, with the yellow "Shocker" mascot on the front.

"Probably be the only kid in California with one of those. Might even get you some attention from the girls." As soon as he said it, he looked over at Mal, who was frowning a little, and grinned. "Maybe it'll work here in Kansas, too."

That night after supper, Mal treated me to a movie and ice cream after. The movie was called "Rosemary's Baby." It was a very creepy horror movie about a young married couple living in an apartment in New York City. They meet some older neighbors who seem nice at first, but gradually begin to take emotional control of Rosemary, the young wife. In the end, Rosemary, does have a baby, though in the final scene, when the audience finally gets to see the baby, whatever it is, is not quite human.

On Monday, Grandpa took me over to the driver's license testing station. When we first got there, it looked like things weren't going to work out, since my birth certificate was back in California. But I had my California learner's permit, which showed my date of birth, and because Grandpa was a judge and just about everybody in the county knew him, the clerk at the license bureau took his word that I was actually a resident of the state of Kansas.

Since I had read the manual and since both Mal and Grandpa reviewed the sample questions with me several times, the written portion of the test was easy, and I got all the questions right. There was a vision test where I had to look into a viewer and identify what I saw, including various road signs like "yield" or "railroad crossing," but without any letters on them. The idea was to be able to say what the signs represented from just their shape and color. There was also a test to determine whether I was color blind. That involved looking at a web of crisscrossed lines and picking out a word hidden in the web. People who were red-green colorblind saw one word, people who were not saw another.

Finally, there was the actual driving test, and for that I had to drive Grandpa's Cadillac while an examiner rode next to me in the passenger seat. The test took about fifteen minutes and the instructor had me make left turns, right turns, stop at stop signs, back out of a parking space and, finally, parallel park between two orange traffic cones. During the drive I was careful to stay under the speed limit because I knew if I went even a mile or two over, the examiner was liable to fail me for committing a violation. I was also extra-conscious of the need to make a complete stop at stop signs, rather than rolling slowly past. At the first stop sign we came to I noticed the examiner held his pen upright and sighted along the side of it to make sure it didn't move in relation to the stop sign. And just to be sure he didn't make a mistake I tapped the brake a little harder, so that the car rocked back slightly when we stopped moving.

When the test was over, I passed, but not with a perfect score, because it took me a couple of tries to get the parallel parking right. I also forgot to use the turn signal once when we were changing lanes. Then, while we waited for my license to be printed, Grandpa told me that he had added me to his insurance policy. He also handed me a brand-new set of keys to his Cadillac. "That way, if you need to go someplace, you won't have to come looking for me or Mary Alice to drive you. You can just go wherever you want."

But where, I wondered, would that be.

CHAPTER THIRTY-SIX

Eight teams from our district made the end-of-season baseball tournament. Seven of them had better records than the Copperheads, so we were seeded eighth and slated to play our first game against a team from Wellington, a town about halfway between Goldenrod and Wichita. The game was to be played at a park district field on the far south side of Wichita, and because the top-seeded Wellington Wildcats had a 13-1 record compared to our 9-5, they were designated the home team.

On the bus ride heading to Wichita, Coach Curtis went over our starting lineup, which was pretty much the same one we had been going with for the last several games: Conrad was starting on the mound, with Robbie behind the plate. The outfield from left to right was Dennis Smith, Larry Griggs and Joe West. The only switch was moving Andy Roselli from short to third, trading places with Eddie Wilson. The rest of the infield was Dave Gomez at second and Junior Hanks at first. Johnny Melendez would be first out of the bullpen and I would finish up if I was needed.

"No matter how it goes today, everybody plays. This is a tournament game, but nobody on this bus gets paid to play baseball, and tournament chances don't come around every day. That makes this one a little bit special for all of us, so I'll do my best to see to it that each of you gets in at least a couple of innings, okay?"

When nobody said anything, he continued. "That said, these guys we're facing today are damn good. They outscored everybody they played by six runs or more, except for the one game they lost, which I don't know how that happened. So, no matter what you brought with you today, I expect you to leave every bit of it on the field, 'cause if we don't get it right today, there's not going to be any tomorrow as far as this season is concerned, got it?"

We got it, and in fact, we did get a few things right that day. First, nobody fell down the steps getting off the bus. Nobody forgot to bring his glove, everybody had on a uniform, and nobody got hurt taking warmups. In the first inning, we even broke out on top thanks to a single by our leadoff man, Andy Roselli. After Dave Gomez walked, Larry Griggs singled, scoring Andy from second, and when the Wildcats center fielder missed the cutoff man with his return throw to the infield, Dave Gomez also came around. Then, with Larry standing on second and nobody out, right fielder Dave Clyde hit a high popup on the infield, which their shortstop caught easily. After that, third baseman Eddie Wilson hit a vicious liner right back to the pitcher, who snagged it and threw to second to double up Larry. Two-zip and three down, inning over. We should have had more, I thought, but at least we were off and running.

In the home half of the first, Conrad Schmidt started off like a house afire, setting down the first two Wildcat hitters on a swinging third strike and then a walk, followed by a crafty pickoff move that caught the overeager runner in no-man's land between first and second. And that's when the wheels came off. Before we were able to close out the inning, the Wildcats came to life and batted around, scoring five runs and leaving a runner stranded at second. After that, it got worse.

The 'Cats pitcher set us down in order in the second and third innings, and only Dennis Smith getting hit by a pitch in the fourth got us a base runner. Meanwhile, Conrad coughed up two more runs in the third and was yanked in favor of Johnny Melendez, who fared no better. In the fourth, guessing that the game would not go seven innings, and with the score already 8-1, Coach kept his promise and pulled several of the starters and replaced them with the guys who hadn't played so far.

By the time I went to the mound in the last of the fifth, it was 10-2, and if we hadn't gotten those two runs in the first, the mercy rule would have taken effect and the game would have been over after four-and-a-half. Even so, I had three outs to get and although it wouldn't make a bit of difference to the outcome of the game, I was going to do my best to get them. And, in fact, I started off pretty well. The first man I faced was the Wildcats first baseman, a left-handed hitter who had already gone three-for-five on the day. He managed to work me all the way to a 3-2 count before grounding sharply to Dan Berlotti, who had taken over for Eddie Wilson at short. However, their next hitter wasted no time lining a single to center on the first pitch, and with a man on first, the 'Cats manager, deciding, I supposed, that he might as well also empty his bench, sent up a pinch-hitter.

I hadn't paid any attention to the kid during warmups, but as he was taking his practice swings, I noticed that, unlike the other Wildcats players, who all seemed to be big and muscular farm kids apparently used to throwing around hay bales and bench-pressing hogs and cattle over their heads for exercise, this kid was small and slender. From his appearance, I first thought he was Japanese. I knew baseball was popular in Japan and some of their professional teams even had a few American players who had come to the end of their careers here at home and were hoping for one last go-around over there.

Before the kid stepped into the batter's box,

Coach Curtis called time, and he and Robbie and the rest of the infield gathered around me on the mound.

"Guys, you need to stay awake with this little dude. I've seen him before. Some of the other coaches know who he is, too, and all he's going to try to do is bunt. He's quick as a lizard getting down the line and unless you guys on the corners move in tight, if he gets it down, he's going to beat it out. Connor, that means if he lays it down the first base line, you need to get over in a hurry to cover the bag, got it?"

"No problem," I said.

"What is this guy," Junior asked, "some Jap?"

"Not hardly," Coach said. "Lineup card says his name is Tran or something like that. He's Vietnamese. He came over a couple years ago as a refugee. I don't know how he wound up in Kansas, except that I heard some church group sponsored him. Anyway, Connor, you don't have to worry about him even getting it out of the infield. He can't hit a lick except, like I said, he can bunt and run pretty damn fast."

"Let's get this guy, Connor," Robbie said as he handed me the ball. "Maybe we can double him up and get out of here. I'm ready to go home."

"Yeah, me too," I said, but I wasn't really

listening to Robbie. The instant I heard the word 'Vietnamese,' my thoughts turned completely away from the game situation and I became one hundred percent focused on the hitter. At that moment, we were the only two people on the field, or for that matter, on the entire earth. And I didn't need to check signals with Robbie to know exactly how I was going to pitch to him.

With a runner on first, I had to work out of the stretch, and, sure enough, as soon as I came to a set position, Tran squared around in the box to bunt. I threw the ball as hard as I could, straight at his head. He saw it coming and ducked out of the way, landing on his butt in the dirt. He got up and dusted himself off, then stepped back into the box. On the next pitch, he squared around again, and again, I threw at his head, this time nearly hitting him. Robbie called time and walked slowly out to the mound. But he didn't hand me the ball.

"This got something to do with your father?" he asked me. "What are you trying to do here, win the Vietnam war?"

"Ball just got away from me," I said.

"I don't think so, Connor. You didn't all of a sudden forget how to pitch."

"Just give me the damn ball, Robbie."

"No. No way. Not unless you tell me you're going to play the game right. This kid didn't have anything to do with what happened to your dad, and if you even look like you're going to throw at him again, I'll call time and tell the ump what you're doing and have him kick you out of the game. Is that how you want to end the season?"

"The ball," I said.

"Okay, but don't do something you're going to regret." Robbie dropped the ball into my glove and walked back behind the plate. And in the few seconds it took him to get into position behind home plate, I came to a decision. Robbie was right. What I was doing was both pointless and wrong.

On the next pitch, Tran again squared around again to bunt and this time I threw a changeup right down the middle. Sure enough, he laid the ball down in a perfect spot about fifteen feet in front of home plate, and before either Robbie or I could get to it to throw down to Junior, Tran was across the bag at first. As I walked back to the mound, I looked right at him, then touched my finger to the bill of my cap.

Five minutes later, the game was over, as the Wildcats loaded the bases on a called ball four that should have been a strike, and then their next hitter crushed a mistake pitch over the left-field fence for a grand slam. That made the score 14-2, and it was game and season over, along with my own string of fairly effective outings.

After the customary round of handshakes and "good-luck" wishes from us to the Wildcats, we began gathering up our equipment and heading back to the bus for the forty-minute ride back to Goldenrod. As I was getting on, I noticed the Vietnamese kid, Tran, walking toward our bus. I went over to meet him, at first thinking he was looking for a fight.

If he wants to hit me, I thought, I'm going to let him.

But fighting wasn't what was on his mind. "You try to hit me on purpose." There was no anger in his voice. "Why?"

"You're from Vietnam, right?"

"Ah," he said, "so, this is about war?"

I said, "My father is a Navy pilot. He flies combat missions. His plane was shot down over North Vietnam a couple months ago."

"He was killed?"

"We don't know. We haven't heard anything definite."

"And you think if you hit me with baseball, war will end and your father will come back." He nodded slowly. "I understand. I am here in United States because my family all die in attack on my village by American airplanes. I was not at my home when bombers came. Otherwise, I would be dead, too. We were not communists. Our village did not support Viet Cong. Later, our government say the attack was a mistake. They apologize and give money to those who survive, but everyone else still dead." His English was not perfect, but his meaning was clear.

"I'm sorry," I said after a moment. "What I did was wrong. Please forgive me."

He nodded. "When I first arrive in America, I was angry. Wanted to hurt somebody for what happen to my family. But the people I am staying with are good people, and after while I understand that in war, other good people sometimes do things they wish they did not have to do. Today, I think, you see what I mean." He stood for a moment, seeming to study my face. And then he turned and walked away. And I was ashamed.

Before we started for home, Coach Curtis got up in the front of the bus and gave us a short speech about how proud he was of us and how we'd had a pretty good season despite the outcome of this particular game.

"Guys, including today, we went 9-6 this year, and that's a .600 winning percentage. It was just luck of the draw that we got a very tough team in the first round. If we'd won one of those close losses earlier in the season, we would have had a different opponent today and things might have turned out better." I noticed he was looking straight at me when he got to that part.

"But even though the score wasn't close, all of you played your asses off out there and kept your cool today, which isn't easy when you get thumped like we did. I'm proud of every one of you."

After the coach's wrap-up, it was a quiet trip home. Most of the guys chose to sit by themselves, except for Robbie, who slid into the seat across the aisle from me near the back of the bus. After a while, he said, "You think you'd feel any better if we'd lost by one run?"

"I'd feel worse."

"I think I would, too. We came, we got clobbered, we went home. This way at least, there aren't any 'what-ifs.' Hey, what'd that Vietnamese kid want just now?"

"He wanted to know why I tried to take his head off."

"What did you tell him?"

"I told him it wasn't on purpose. I said he was so small I couldn't see him behind his bat."

"Good answer," he said, grinning. "Hey, I heard you got your driver's license. Now you're free as a bird."

"Yeah, thanks," I said. "Like I've got someplace to go."

"Well, I also heard you're taking Mal to the country club dance. I expect that's someplace, isn't it?”

“Who told you that?”

“Robin. I talked to her after practice the other day. She said Mal is really excited, because she thought for a while you weren’t going to ask her. I think she went and bought a new outfit.”

“So then, are you going with Robin?”

He shook his head. “No. I’m taking Louise. Robin is going with Dennis.”

CHAPTER THIRTY-SEVEN

The middle of August was only a few days away and my time in Goldenrod was about to come to an end. The last time I spoke with Mom during her most recent Sunday call, she said her posting at the hospital in Tokyo would be completed at the end of her shift on Saturday, August thirty-first, and that the next day, September first, she would be on a plane headed back to San Francisco. She said she had already spoken to Grandpa, and that he would call the Santa Fe ticket office in Wichita and reserve a ticket for me on the westbound *San Francisco Chief* departing the day after her plane left Japan. That would put me back in Fresno at the ungodly hour of 5:45 in the morning on the fifth. I was already calculating what time that meant I would have to be up and dressed in time for my arrival, but considering that I was finally going home, it really didn't matter much about the time. Besides, sleeping on a moving train, even if it was in a bed, was a skill I was a long way from perfecting.

"So, I'll see you in Fresno on Thursday, the fifth," Mom said. "We can go and get breakfast anywhere you like." (Welcome news, since the dining car on the train did not open until 6:00 A.M.) "And I think I'll have couple of surprises for you." And I'd have a surprise for her, too, when she found out I had a driver's license.

On one hand, I was excited to be going back home, and to reconnect with my California friends. Since Labor Day was on the second, school would have already started by the time I got back, but I wasn't worried about missing the first couple of days. Nothing much happens the first week anyway, as teachers are busy handing out books and figuring out seating charts to keep the problem people separated from one another.

On the other hand, and to be perfectly honest, there was a lot I was going to miss about Goldenrod, including Grandpa and a few of my baseball friends like Robbie and Junior. But I was especially going to miss Mal. Saying good-bye to her was not going to be easy. At the same time, I was worried about Grandpa. I assumed he would make arrangements for someone to drive him back and forth to Wichita for his cancer treatments, but he hadn't said anything about it so far. I guessed the likeliest choice for a driver would be Mrs. Mueller, since she was coming to the house most days anyway.

But more than who wondering who might be doing the driving, I was also concerned—no, I was scared—about his overall condition, which, if I had to judge from his appearance, was getting worse. He was still coughing, and since Grandpa had begun his treatments, he had lost a lot of weight. I knew this wasn't unusual for patients undergoing cancer treatments, because the chemo often leaves them feeling nauseated and unable to keep food down. But considering that he wasn't carrying around a lot of extra pounds to begin with, losing much more weight would leave him weakened generally and make fighting his disease that much more difficult. Worse yet, he was beginning to talk as if he had already given up, saying things like, "When I'm not here anymore," and "After I'm gone."

And then there was the dance, which was coming up on Saturday night, just five days away. Grandpa said he thought it would be a good idea if I got a haircut, since I hadn't had one since before leaving Fresno. He said I was beginning to look like a beach bum. Mal agreed, emphatically. Grandpa also said, since he found out boys were expected to wear jackets and ties, that we should go into town and buy me a new sport coat.

"I notice that one you brought with you doesn't fit quite right. Guess you haven't had to wear it in a while. You want to look good when they start taking pictures." So, on Wednesday, a day when we didn't need to go to Wichita, Grandpa went into town with me, where first I got a haircut, which was a lot shorter than I wanted, and then to both the Sears store and Montgomery-Ward, looking for a jacket that Grandpa thought would be appropriate for the dance.

"'Course, if you want, there's a men's store in Wichita we can check on after we finish up at the clinic."

"I don't think we need to do that," I told him. "I just need something that fits. I'm sure we can find something here." And we did, a navy-blue blazer, along with a white shirt and a red-and-blue necktie.

"Those girls at the dance will all be lining up to get a turn around the floor with you," Grandpa said. "You'll be the best-dressed young man in the clubhouse." I wasn't sure about that, but when I checked myself out in the mirror in the men's department, I had to admit I looked pretty sharp.

When Grandpa and I got back from town, Mrs. Mueller told me that Robbie Curtis had called, and could I call him back right away?

"I need a favor," he said, when he came on the line. "You still going to the dance on Saturday with Mal?"

"That's the plan," I told him.

"Okay, can I get a ride with you? I mean, you've got your license. You are driving, right? Mal's not taking the Crapmobile?"

"No, no Crapmobile. We're taking my grandfather's car," I said, remembering the driving-to-work-only limitation Grandpa had put on Robbie's license. "Oh, that's right. You're still 'a-walkin'' until school starts. I forgot about that. Sure, that's no problem. I guess then we'll have to go get Louise, too, or does she already have a ride?"

There was a pause. "I sort of told her we'd pick her up."

"Sort of?"

"Okay, I said we'd pick her up. Is that a problem?"

"Not a bit. But how come you aren't hitching a ride with Dennis? Don't you two usually hang out together?"

Robbie sighed. "It's like this. Dennis told Robin who told Louise who told me that he's planning to bring some hard stuff to the dance. I don't want to be in the car with him if he's drinking like that. That's sure to end up being trouble. Plus, I could end up losing my license all over again."

"Got it. Pick you up at seven-thirty," I said, and hung up.

I spent the rest of the afternoon washing the Cadillac and vacuuming the inside until the car looked like it had just rolled off the end of the assembly line. Then, because it was a hot and humid day, I prayed that we wouldn't get an unexpected thunderstorm or a sudden wind that would stir up a bunch of dust and ruin all the work I had done. For Mal, and for me, I wanted this night to be as perfect as I could make it.

CHAPTER THIRTY-EIGHT

Before I left the house to pick up Robbie, and then Mal and Louise, Grandpa called me into the living room to stand for inspection. He straightened my tie and brushed a spot of lint off my jacket before pronouncing me fit to be seen in public with, as he said, a very nice young lady who deserved the best.

"And one more thing. I know you know better, but I also know how things go sometimes. No matter what else is going on at that dance, I don't want to find out you were smoking any pot, or doing any drinking, like that other time. You're not only responsible for yourself, but for the other three people in the car. Anything bad happens while you're driving, you will never forgive yourself, understand?"

"Yes," I promised. "No beer."

"And no anything else, either. I mean it. You slip up, you find a phone and call me, and we'll see to it everybody gets home safe." And with Grandpa's admonition ringing in my ears, I headed out for what was to be an evening to remember.

Turned out, we didn't have to pick up Louise. She had worked it out with Mal that her mom and dad would drop her at Mal's house and then they'd all wait there for Robbie and me so that both sets of parents could take photos before we headed over to the country club. I told Mal they didn't have to bother, and that I could just as easily pick up everybody on my way to her house, but she said it didn't matter what I wanted. All the parents wanted pictures, and that's all there was to it. It didn't mean that much to me to have my picture taken, but then, I often don't understand why some things are as important to parents as they seem to be.

And yet, despite my earlier feelings, I was glad for the photos. Mal looked absolutely beautiful in a royal blue dress, blue shoes and a hairdo that had probably taken most of the afternoon to get just right. The impression was even more striking when I realized that, except for the day we were all in court, I had never seen her wearing anything other than jeans or shorts and a t-shirt or a blouse, and that included the night at Louise's party. For her part, Louise looked just as nice in a pink and white rose print dress and red shoes. Seeing the two of them together made me think that tonight, Robbie and I would be dancing with the prettiest girls in Sunflower County, if not the entire state of Kansas.

"Wow," I said. "You look beautiful. Both of you." But I was looking straight at Mal when I said it.

Before we left for the dance, Dr. Mueller

gave what I was coming to understand was the standard grownup pep talk about driving carefully, not drinking, not smoking, and not trying to set any land-speed records with Grandpa's Cadillac. Also, Mr. Porter said, no "hanky-panky," as he called it, in the back seat, to which Louise responded, "Da-a-a-a-d."

I assured Dr. Mueller that Grandpa had laid down the same rules before I left the house. I promised that I would be absolutely careful with my driving, and that we would all be on our best behavior. As far as afterward, Louise had already let her parents know that there would probably be a few kids who would be hosting parties at their homes after the dance ended, and that we might stop at one of them before heading for home.

"Home by twelve-thirty, no later," said Mrs. Porter. "Got that? Louise? Connor? Everybody?"

"Loud and clear," I said, and by the time we were all settled in the car and on our way, I had come to the realization that the entire evening had been mapped and scheduled some time earlier by Mal and Louise, and that Robbie and I were just there because the girls didn't want to go to the dance by themselves.

Thanks to the time spent getting our pictures taken, the dance had already started by the time we got to the country club, and we could hear music streaming out the front door as we pulled into the parking lot. I dropped Robbie and the girls at the entrance and went to find a place to park. I was careful to find a spot as far away as possible from the other cars and trucks in the lot. I wanted to make sure I wouldn't be bringing Grandpa's car back to him with dings in the doors.

Robbie had already bought all our tickets, which were five dollars apiece, when I got back from parking the car. I reached for my wallet to pay him my ten dollars, but he said, "Forget it. It was worth it to watch you drive like you were a hundred years old. And besides, I got to sit in the back with Louise," a remark that promptly got him a pair of raised eyebrows from Mal and a sharp elbow in his ribs from his date.

Inside the main room, there were tables and chairs set up for eight as well as three long tables where the country club wait staff was serving sodas and lemonade as well as cookies, chips, pizza and other snacks. At the far end of the room was a platform where a disc jockey dressed in a tuxedo sat between two of the tallest speaker-towers I had ever seen. He had two turntables, so he didn't have to pause the music between records. As soon as one song was winding down, he had another already cued up on the second turntable.

Looking around, I recognized several people

from Louise's party, as well as all but two of the guys from the baseball team. Robbie told me the two who were missing, Eddie Wilson and Joe West, were members of some church that frowned on dancing and rock and roll music, and so their parents had kept them home.

As soon as we found places to sit down, Mal grabbed me by the hand and led me from one table to the next, greeting her friends and introducing me to the ones I hadn't met. Then it was off to the dance floor. I tried my best to keep up, but it was obvious that Mal knew all the latest dances. On the other hand, I did not, and it showed. I tried to follow some of her steps, and she even took a shot at coaching me a little, but despite my best efforts, I mostly ended up lurching clumsily around like my shoes weighed ten pounds apiece.

Eventually, though, the deejay played a few slow songs, and I was able to find enough of a rhythm that at least I didn't step on Mal's feet or embarrass either one of us. Plus, it was exciting holding her close to me as we moved to the music, and in the few minutes it took to play those songs, I found myself wishing there were a way I could stay in Goldenrod forever.

The deejay announced that he was going to take a short break, so Mal and I went back to our table, where Robbie and Louise were sitting, talking to Robin. Dennis was there, too, but he wasn't talking to anybody. And when he saw Mal and me holding hands as we approached, the look on his face turned dark and angry.

"My favorite people," he said, slurring his words just slightly. Obviously, he had already gotten started drinking whatever it was he had brought with him.

"You two having a good time?" Robin had a stricken look on her face, as if she had realized that accepting an invitation from Dennis had been a mistake, and that she was sure something was about to go seriously wrong.

Before I had a chance to say anything, Mal spoke up. "We're doing just fine, Denny, and please don't do something stupid to spoil things for everybody."

Dennis looked at Mal for a long moment without saying anything, and it seemed to me that in that interval, the look in his eyes changed from anger to sadness. Then he got up and walked unsteadily away from the table and out the front door. Nobody followed him.

CHAPTER THIRTY-NINE

Robin looked like she was ready burst into tears at any moment.

"He had already been drinking when he picked me up," she said. "But he didn't come into the house, he just pulled into the driveway and honked his horn. I'm sure he knew that if my parents got a look at him, they wouldn't have let me go."

"They shouldn't have," Louise said. "And Robin, you should have known better than to get into the car with him."

"I know," she said, "but I wanted to come tonight. It's the last thing before the end of the summer, and I knew once I found you and Mal, I could get away from him and still have a good time. I figured I could get a ride home with one of you if I had to."

"Did he say anything on the way over?" Mal asked.

"No, not really, just . . . Connor, he's awfully mad at you. I don't know why for sure, but I don't think it has anything to do with baseball."

Just then, the music started up again. The deejay cued up "How Can I Be Sure," a slow song that was popular just about a year earlier.

"Come on, Connor," Mal said, taking my

hand. "I love this song."

As we got up to dance, I heard Robbie tell Louise he was going to go outside and see what happened to Robbie. "Be right back," he said. "I just want to make sure he's okay. He's liable to do something really stupid out there by himself."

Mal and I danced our dance, very close and very slowly, and then the deejay turned things around and played a song called "Boogaloo Down Broadway," which had its own steps to go with it. Mal tried to show me what to do, but I just wasn't getting the hang of it, and after about thirty seconds, she laughed and said she'd seen enough. "Okay, let's go sit down."

When we got back to the table, Robbie was sitting by himself. Mal asked what happened to Robin and Louise, and Robbie said when he came back inside after checking on Dennis, Robin had gotten herself all worked up and started crying, so Louise went with her to the ladies' room to try to settle her down. When Mal heard that, she announced she was going to check up on Robin and Louise.

I said to Robbie, "So, did you find Dennis?"

"Yeah, I did."

"Is he okay?"

"Depends on what you call okay. He's got a baseball bat. He's over by your grandfather's car and he says he's going to break out all the windows if you don't come out and fight him. I don't know what's going on with him. He's got some kind of a problem with you and he wants to settle it right now." He waited, and when I didn't say anything right away, he said, "What are you going to do?"

"Go see what he wants, I guess."

"You want me to go with you?"

"No, this isn't your problem. Besides," I said, with more confidence than I felt, "he's not going to hit me with a bat."

I took off my jacket and hung it over the back of my chair. "But just the same, wait here until the girls come back. Then if you want to, you can come on out and see what's going on. But don't make a thing about it and don't bring the girls with you. I don't think this is going to turn out to be anything, and there's nothing good going to come from having a whole bunch of people standing around egging us on."

I walked out to the empty space next to where I had left Grandpa's Cadillac. Sure enough, there was Dennis with a baseball bat in his hands. His shirt was untucked and his tie was hanging loosely to one side.

"Didn't figure you'd have the guts to show up," he said when he saw me.

"Well, I'm here. Any point in asking, or

before you beat up my grandfather's car, are you going to tell me what's your problem?"

"My problem? My problem is since you got here, nothing has gone right for me. I can't hit a baseball anymore, my girlfriend broke up with me and I got arrested and fined for trespassing and for drinking at a party."

"Let me understand this," I said. "Every morning, all across Sunflower County, roosters crow and the sun comes up. By your logic, the roosters are in charge of the sunrise."

He looked at me, uncomprehending. "What?"

"It doesn't matter," I said. "Look, this doesn't have to happen. Robin is pretty upset, and she's stuck sitting inside by herself. Why don't you just shake it off and go back and dance with her? You're her date and this is a big night for the girls."

"Not just yet," he said, swinging the bat back and forth in the air. "This first dance is just for me and you."

"Okay, I give up. If that's what you want, then come on and bring it. You can even lead."

Dennis tossed the bat on the ground behind him and got into a fighting stance. I expected he was planning to come straight at me and try to land a solid blow to my head or my face. I also knew that he had a good thirty pounds on me and that if he got me down on the ground, I'd be in real trouble. I tried to remember some of the techniques the Marine instructors had taught me for defending myself in a situation where I might be facing a puncher rather than a boxer. I could only come up with one.

I spread my arms the width of my body and kept my hands open, thinking I could either block or deflect his punch. At the same time, I began circling a few steps to my right so that when I had to hit back, I'd have a clear shot with my left.

He came at me the way I thought he would, in a rush, cocking his fist and swinging with all his strength. I just had time to get my arms up in front of my face and body and caught his blow on my forearms. The force of it pushed me a step to the right, which meant my left arm was free and his right side was momentarily undefended. I was off-balance, however, and there wasn't much force behind my own punch, which landed on his left shoulder. I knew a blow like that wouldn't hurt him at all, but it was enough to move him backward a step or two, and that was enough for him to step on the bat. His right foot went out from under him and he fell, landing on his back and hitting his head on the ground. For a moment, he didn't move.

Up until that instant, because I was facing away from the clubhouse, and because I was concentrating so hard on Dennis, I hadn't noticed that Mal, Robin, Louise and about a dozen other kids had followed Robbie out the door to see what was going on. When Dennis tripped and fell on the ground, several of the kids began laughing. It was too much. Dennis, who was more embarrassed than hurt, picked himself up off the ground. And instead of coming after me for round two, he walked slowly over to his car, got in and drove away.

It wasn't until later that night that I learned that just a few minutes after he drove off, Dennis Smith somehow managed to run his car off the road at better than sixty miles an hour and crash head-on into a utility pole.

CHAPTER FORTY

After Dennis drove off, all of us went back inside and sat down. And as expected, those who had come out to see what ended up being a one-punch fight (the one I threw was more like a hard push) wanted to talk about it, and it wasn't long before everyone at the dance heard what had happened. Some came over to talk to me, either to find out more about how I had been able to "beat up Dennis," or to congratulate me for putting an unpopular bully in his place. I tried to deflect as much of that as I could, explaining that Dennis had simply tripped and fallen, and that I hadn't done anything to earn any handshakes or pats on the back. I also didn't mention that Dennis had been drinking before he got to the dance, and therefore was at a disadvantage, though I doubted he was thinking about that when he decided to call me out.

After some coaxing, Mal was able to get me back on the dance floor, and I was even able to manage a poor imitation of some of the steps that went with dances like the Jerk and the Swim. Of course, anybody can do the Twist, and I had no trouble with that. At the end of the evening, the deejay played an extended medley of slow songs, and Mal and I stayed on the floor for every one of them. During those last few dances, I even forgot about Dennis Smith and that, before too many more days passed, I would be on the train heading back to Fresno.

After the end of the dance, the four of us who rode together in Grandpa's car, plus Robin, who had lost her ride when Dennis took off, went to a party at the home of a girl named Kathleen Morris. I remembered meeting Kathleen ("call her Kate") after the game at Blackwell, back in June, when we got blown out by the home-team Braves. There were about twenty kids at Kate's house, still dressed up from the dance, and everybody seemed to be talking about the new school year, which would be starting the following week. The first football game was the Friday after that. Some of the girls had been chosen as cheerleaders and everybody was comparing notes about the classes they would be taking. I told Mal it was okay with me if she wanted to be with her friends instead of sitting on the couch holding hands with me, but she said no, she was just fine where she was.

After a while, a couple guys who hadn't come out to watch the fight I had with Dennis came over to ask me about it, and I realized that the mere fact I had survived the encounter in one piece was a major item of interest. I remembered Grandpa said that over the years, Dennis had gotten into a fair number of fights, and before tonight, had always come out on top. Tonight, though, was a different story, and people had questions. But in my mind, I hadn't done anything to be proud of, and so I told everybody who came asking questions that I was so scared while it was happening that I really didn't remember much. I was also thinking about something one of my Marine instructors had told me when they were teaching me self-defense.

Whether you win or lose the fight, when it's over, you should never disrespect your opponent.

We had been at Kate's house for less than an hour when Robin asked Mal to ask me if it would be okay if we took her home. I could see she wasn't having a very good time, and after Dennis ditched her at the country club, she just wanted to put the whole evening behind her. Besides, it was getting close to twelve-thirty, the time when I promised to have Louise home, so we said goodbye to Kate and the rest of the kids and headed out. And even though Goldenrod is a small town, it seemed like nobody lived close to anybody else, and so it took some time to get everyone back where they belonged. But after dropping off Robin, then Louise, and finally Robbie, Mal and I were alone in Grandpa's car.

"Connor," she asked me on the way back to her house, "I know this is kind of a silly question, but I want to ask you anyway. If there was a way you could stay here in Goldenrod instead of going back to California, would you?"

"It's not silly, and I've thought about the same thing more times than I can count. And yes, if I could, I'd stay forever," I said. "I'm going to miss you a lot."

We drove around for a few more minutes after that, neither of us saying anything. It was well after midnight and the streets were deserted. The houses all around town were dark, and although it was a warm night, I think it was at that moment that we both knew, with complete certainty, that summer was over. In a few days we would be saying goodbye, maybe until next summer, or maybe forever. It was that realization, I understood later, that made the goodnight kiss we exchanged when I walked her to her front door and she went into the house seem all the more precious.

CHAPTER FORTY-ONE

When I got back to Grandpa's house, he was sitting on the front porch swing, a cup of coffee in hand, waiting for me. This was unusual for him, as he generally went to bed early. At first, I thought he wanted to check out his car to make sure I hadn't smashed it up during my first after-dark solo drive, but that wasn't what was on his mind.

"So," he said, "did you make soup or just boil water?"

"What?" I had no idea what he was talking about.

"I hear you got into a scuffle with that Smith kid over at the country club."

"You know about that already?" It was amazing how fast he seemed to find out about, well, everything.

"Folks like to tell me things. It goes with the job. Are you okay?"

"I'm fine, Grandpa. And anyway, it wasn't much of a fight. He hit me once, I halfway hit him back and then he tripped and fell and that was the end of it."

"So then, you just warmed up the water a little bit. You sure there's nothing more to it?"

"I didn't say anything before it happened, but there were still some kids at the dance who heard there was going to be a fight, so they came outside to watch. When Dennis fell down, they laughed at him. I guess he was embarrassed. He got in his car and took off. We didn't see him any more after that."

"Well," Grandpa said, "I'm afraid he pretty much crashed on take-off. Right before you got home, the sheriff called and said Dennis Smith ran his car off the road and into line pole. An ambulance came and they took him to county hospital. Sheriff said the car looked bad. They weren't sure about the driver."

I was stunned. "Does that mean he's not going to be okay?"

"Don't know. There was evidence he'd been drinking. They'll do a blood test at the hospital to find out for sure."

"This is my fault," I said. "I never should have gone outside to face him."

Grandpa took a sip of his coffee. "Getting cold," he said and tossed the rest of it over the porch railing. "I'm not saying you're right, but if you think you shouldn't have gone out, why did you?"

"Robbie said Dennis had a baseball bat and he was going to break out all the windows in your car if I didn't come out. Before we fought, he threw it on the ground. It was the bat he tripped over when he fell."

He laughed and stood up to go inside. "And they say there's no justice in the world. Come on, it's late. Tomorrow after we talk to your mom, we'll take a run over to the hospital and see how he's getting along."

Sunday morning, Mom called from Tokyo at her usual time. As had been the case all summer, there was still no word about Dad, just that the Navy was trying to find out whether he was MIA, KIA or POW, but the North Vietnamese were not willing to give out any information. As far as they were concerned, all captured American pilots had committed war crimes, and so they had no right to expect to being treated as anything other than criminals.

"I got confirmation that my posting is up on the thirty-first," she said. "I'll be flying home on the first, and I'll meet you at the train station on the fifth. Got your ticket yet?"

"No, we're going to do that on Tuesday, when we go to Wichita."

There was a pause. "How's Grandpa doing?"

"About the same," I said. "He's still coughing a lot and Mrs. Mueller says she's finding blood on his pillowcases and towels."

"Okay," she said, "let me talk to him. I'm not going to call next week because I'll be in transit, so you take care and I'll see you soon. I love you. I miss you."

"Love you too, Mom," I said, and handed the phone to Grandpa. Then I went upstairs to take a shower and get dressed for a visit to the hospital.

Sunflower County Hospital was located out on the state highway, about a mile south of downtown. The volunteer lady behind the reception desk told us Dennis was in a room on the second floor. There were two beds in the room, she said, but unless more people turned up sick before he was able to go home, Dennis had the room to himself.

When we went into his room, Dennis was awake and in bed, looking out the window. The television was turned off. His right leg was in a cast and was elevated to prevent swelling in his foot and ankle. His right hand and wrist were also in a cast, and there were dark bruises on the side of his face and around his eyes. A bandage covered his forehead where he had taken some stiches. Laying in bed the way he was, he somehow looked smaller than what I remembered from the previous night.

"Morning, youngster," Grandpa said when we entered Dennis's room. "I figured we'd have to fight our way through a crowd of pretty girls and a mountain of flowers just to get through the door."

"Hey, Judge," Dennis said. His voice

sounded groggy. "Didn't expect to see you 'til the sheriff put the cuffs on me and dragged me back into the courtroom."

"We'll have plenty of time for that later," Grandpa said. "I brought Connor along, in case you two hooligans wanted to finish your fight, but I expect that'll have to wait for a while. Incidentally, thanks for not breaking out the windows in my car. That glass is expensive."

"Aw, Judge, you know I never would have really busted your windows. I respect you way too much to do a thing like that.

"I wonder. Where's your family, by the way?"

"Church, probably prayin' I don't live through this. Pop's pretty mad right now."

"Can't say I blame him," Grandpa said. "Anybody else been by to see you?"

"Not since last night. Say, Judge, what's going to happen to me when they let me out of here? Am I going to go to the county lockup?"

"Doubt it. Sheriff charged you with a couple of traffic violations. Driving under the influence—guess you know what that means—and operating a motor vehicle in an unsafe manner. You'll end up with a healthy fine and a suspended license, but that shouldn't be much of a problem for you, since I hear your car is a total loss. Either way, we can sort all that out later. Important thing now is that you get mended and then you need to get busy cleaning up your act. That baseball team is going to need you next summer."

Grandpa looked at his watch. "Connor, I've got to talk to somebody downstairs. How about you meet me in the lobby in about ten minutes. Give you boys a few minutes by yourselves. I know you've got things to talk about."

After Grandpa left, I pulled a chair around to the left side of Dennis's bed, where he could see me without having to turn over onto his injured side.

"I guess you came by to tell me what a dumbass I am."

I laughed at that. "Do you really need somebody to point that out?"

"No, I guess not. Doctor says I'm gonna be laid up for close to a month and then there'll be therapy. I'll have plenty of time to think things over."

"Maybe not a bad thing, but it sounds like you'll be good to go for next season."

There was a pause. Then I said, "Dennis, can I ask you something?"

"Sure, why not? It's ain't like I'm gonna jump out of bed and pound you."

"Just this. It seems like from the time I got here, you've had some kind of a problem with me. I can't figure out why, and I'm going back to California at the end of the week, so I won't have another chance to ask. I mean, I remember what you said last night, but I didn't have anything to do with any of that stuff you were talking about. It couldn't have been because I struck you out that first day we met, could it?"

He shook his head, which must have hurt because he winced and drew a sharp breath. "I didn't care about that. I mean, I'm not used to getting fooled that way, but we don't hardly face any lefthanders in this league. Anyway, I would have gotten around to lighting you up after I saw a few more pitches.

"What got me was that next day when I saw you sitting in the car with Mal at the drive-in. I mean, I've been crazy about her for a long time. I know I didn't do right by her, but I thought she might get over it and we could patch things up after a while. But then, here you come, looking like you could be one of the Beach Boys, and the longer you were here, the more it seemed like she thought everything you did was just perfect. And I knew then, I'd never get her back, so I blamed you for stealing her away from me instead of blaming myself for how I acted."

"You know, I hear that all the time at school about how somebody stole somebody else's girlfriend or boyfriend. But it seems to me the only time somebody gets stolen is when they're tired of who they're with and they're ready to move on."

"I know. Pretty stupid, huh?"

I had to smile at that. "You mean stupid like me thinking I could win the damn war by beaning that Vietnamese kid?"

"Yeah, I wondered about that," he said, and for the first time, his voice softened just a little. "I knew you had better control than that."

"I blamed him for what happened to my dad. But then I talked to him after the game. He told me his whole family was killed in a bombing raid, which is why he's here in the U.S. and not still in Vietnam."

He nodded. "It doesn't feel good being a shit, does it, Connor?"

"No, it doesn't."

"So, you're for sure going home this week?"

"Yep. My train leaves Saturday night."

He gave me a wide grin. "Too bad. I would have liked to face you again. I'll bet I could take you yard, no problem."

"In your dreams," I told him. "I'd smoke you every time." Then we laughed and shook hands and I went downstairs to find Grandpa.

CHAPTER FORTY-TWO

I didn't see much of Mal the next few days. On Monday she dropped her mom at Grandpa's house and then took off in the Crapmobile before I could get downstairs to talk to her. That afternoon, Dr. Mueller picked up his wife on his way home from the veterinary clinic, so I missed her that time, too. I thought about calling, but then it occurred to me that maybe Mal felt uncomfortable about what she had said to me on Saturday night after the dance and didn't want to talk to me, so I let it go.

On Tuesday, and on Thursday this time, since the Labor Day weekend was coming up and the clinic would be closed on Friday, Grandpa and I went to Wichita for his therapy. He said he wasn't feeling well, and so I drove both ways. On the way to the clinic on Tuesday, we stopped at the train station and picked up my ticket for Fresno. From there, we drove to the clinic where I waited with Grandpa while he was being treated. I couldn't put my finger on just exactly how, but it seemed like every time he got another dose of chemo, he came home looking worse. Compared to when I arrived in June, he for sure had lost a lot of weight and he was walking much more slowly, as if each step he took was painful. The coughing hadn't stopped, either, and it was becoming harder for him to keep down what little food he managed to eat.

On Wednesday, Mal again dropped off her mom and then immediately drove away. I asked Mrs. Mueller if something was wrong, and was Mal upset with me for some reason, but she said no, that Mal had an errand to run that might take the rest of the afternoon. And since Grandpa had a hearing at the courthouse that morning, I was stuck with nothing to do except work in the yard and go for a bike ride.

Finally, on Friday, Mal came to the house with her mom. I was sitting on the front porch swing when they drove up, and after Mrs. Mueller went into the house to start her housekeeping chores, Mal came and sat down next to me. She handed me a shopping bag with the name of a department store on it, and said, "I brought you something."

I looked inside the bag. There was a large brown envelope and a flat box that felt heavy.

"I made you some brownies to take on the train. You don't have to open that now but look at what's in the envelope."

I found two photos inside. One showed Robbie, Louise, Mal and me together at the Porters' house just before we left for the dance. The other picture was just Mal and me, standing close, she in her new dress and me in the navy-blue blazer, white shirt and tie Grandpa bought for me.

"There's nowhere here in Goldenrod to get them developed without having to wait for a week, but there's a camera store in Wellington, so I took the film up there on Monday. I wanted to wait, but they said they couldn't get them developed and enlarged on the same day, so I had to go back yesterday and pick them up."

"Thank you," I said, feeling suddenly sad. "Soon as I get home, I'll buy a couple of frames and put them in my bedroom."

"Will you keep them forever?"

"Longer than that. Will I see you tomorrow before I leave?"

"No. That's why I brought you this stuff today." She hesitated, as if the words she was looking for lay just beyond her reach.

"Connor, I can't go with you to Wichita and then watch the train pull out, knowing I might never see you again. It would break my heart to say goodbye like that. I'd rather remember you and me together, right here, right now, and then maybe I can tell myself that then next time I come over to help my mom, you'll still be here, waiting for me on the porch.

"I remember I told you a story, and I promised that if it didn't come true, I'd have another one for you, but I don't. Right now, I just—

Connor, I've never said this to a boy before, but I love you and I can't bear the thought of you not being here every day for the rest of my life."

"I love you, too, Mal," I told her. And then she kissed me and we said goodbye.

CHAPTER FORTY-THREE

On Saturday evening, I loaded my sea bag and my overnight case into the trunk of Grandpa's car and we took off for Wichita. The train wasn't scheduled to arrive until eleven o'clock at night, which meant that, after dropping me off, Grandpa would be driving back to Goldenrod very late and by himself. I was worried about that and suggested that he ask Mrs. Mueller or one of the off-duty deputies from the court to come along. But since he was a day and a half past his last chemo treatment on Thursday morning, he said he was feeling okay, and that I shouldn't be concerned.

"You got plenty of other things to think about," he told me. "You need to be helping your mom. She's got a big load to carry without your dad. And you should write to Mary Alice once in a while. I think she's going to miss you."

And I'm going to miss her, I thought.

"What about your treatment visits? How are you going to handle getting there and back?"

"Loretta Mueller said she'd come along and do some of the driving. She's getting paid anyway, so she won't be missing out on her money."

"Grandpa, you know I didn't really want to be here, not because of you, but I was looking forward to summer at home."

He looked at me. "Is there a 'however' in that?"

"Yes," I said. "I actually had a pretty good time. And not just for teaching me how to drive, I'm glad I came."

"I'm glad you did, too."

"Only please get better soon. I don't want this to be the last time I see you."

"I'll do my best," he told me.

We got to Wichita about ten-thirty, only to find out the train was delayed loading mail in Kansas City, and so it was nearly midnight by the time it got to the station. When it was finally ready for boarding, Grandpa walked out to the platform with me where the conductor checked my ticket, then pointed me in the direction of my sleeping car. The porter checked my ticket a second time, then asked whether I wanted to check my sea bag in the baggage car, or since I had a bedroom going home, which was larger than the space I had coming east, would I like to stow it in my room. I said in my room would be fine, and he said he'd bring it and make down my bed once we were underway.

"Well, I guess this is so long for a while," Grandpa said as I boarded. "Maybe you and your mom can come visit at Christmastime."

"I'd like that," I said. "I'll bet she would, too."

The train ride back to California was like seeing the first trip in reverse. I slept through the overnight part of the run through western Kansas, western Oklahoma, the Texas panhandle and the eastern part of New Mexico before my eyes popped open somewhere past Clovis. After breakfast in the dining car, which I had to pay for myself, since there were no generous Army officers seated at my table, I spent of the rest of the day in the dome lounge watching out the window as the *San Francisco Chief* rolled through the New Mexico and Arizona deserts. I skipped lunch in the diner and instead filled up on chips and Cokes until it started to get dark.

When I went back to my room after supper, the porter came by and asked if I'd like my bed made down early.

"We're scheduled into Fresno at five forty-five, so you'll probably want me to give you a wake-up call 'bout five. That be all right with you?"

Oh, man, five in the morning. That meant Mom would have to be up about that same hour to get to the station in time to meet the train when it arrived.

"Sure. Just give me time to get cleaned up before we get in."

I stepped out into the corridor while the porter made down my bed, then went back into the bedroom where I got undressed and crawled under the covers. Unlike the previous night, I had trouble falling asleep. I was thinking about Mal and Grandpa and Dad and starting school the week after I got back, and pretty soon the inside of my head was buzzing like there was a swarm of bees inside. And it seemed like no sooner had I dozed off when the porter was knocking on my door. During the night, he told me, the train had made up most of the time lost in Kansas City, and we would only be a few minutes late arriving in Fresno.

"Otherwise, I'd a' let you sleep a little longer."

There was no shower in my bedroom, so I got washed up the best way I could, put on clean clothes and got out of the way so the porter could make up the room. It was just beginning to get light outside when the train slowed, then rolled to a stop at the Fresno depot. Mom was already there, waiting and smiling.

"I missed you," she said, after a long hug. "Let me look at you. Are you okay?"

"I'm fine, Mom. I missed you, too."

Another hug, then, "I've got lots to tell you, and I'll bet you're hungry. Come on, let's go get some breakfast and we can get caught up."

CHAPTER FORTY-FOUR

On the way to the restaurant Mom talked about her residency at the hospital in Japan, and about some of the interesting cases she's never seen before, including jellyfish stings and various infections and stomach problems arising from U. S. soldiers trying to eat weird stuff like *fugu* (puffer fish), tuna eyeballs, and *iki ikizukuri*, which is squid, sliced while it's still alive so that, if it's done right, you can feel its tentacles still wiggling when you put it in your mouth.

When I said I didn't want to hear any more about that, she shifted gears and began asking about my stay in Goldenrod. I skipped over the parts about getting into a fight and almost getting arrested for underage drinking at Louise's party. I figured if I was lucky, Grandpa wouldn't bring it up during one of his phone calls with Mom. I did tell her about playing baseball, and about going crow hunting with Robbie and Junior.

"Really," she said, laughing out loud, "The both got poison ivy?"

"Yeah. It was pretty bad. Bad enough that they couldn't play in our next game, but it didn't matter because the team we were playing wasn't any good and we won anyway."

"Lucky you didn't get it, too." There was a

pause. "Your grandpa says you met a girl. Mary Alice is her name, is that right?"

I nodded. "The kids all call her Mal. Her dad is a veterinarian and her mother is Grandpa's housekeeper. Mal comes with her most days to help. We got to know each other pretty well, since she was there almost every day."

Mom shot me questioning look. "How well is pretty well?"

"You don't have to worry, Mom," I said, taking her meaning. "Nothing happened."

"Okay. And how about your grandfather? How is he really doing?"

"You're the doctor, Mom. You talked to him," I said, hoping to avoid giving her an answer.

She let it go for the moment and didn't ask any more questions until we got to the restaurant and got seated in a booth. After the waitress took our order, Mom took a small package wrapped in birthday paper out of her purse and handed it to me.

"I'll bet you thought I forgot. Happy birthday. I didn't want to mail it, because I wasn't sure how long it would take getting through customs, and because I wanted to give it to you myself." She gave me a big smile. "Go ahead, open it."

I tore off the paper and found a box marked with Japanese pictograms. Underneath, in English, was the name of a jewelry store in Tokyo. Inside was a very expensive-looking gold wristwatch.

"These are supposed to be some of the best in the world. I got it at a store in the Ginza shopping district, in Tokyo. Seiko means 'exquisite' in Japanese. It's self-winding, so you don't have to remember to wind it every day." She waited while I put it on my right wrist.

"Do you like it?"

"It's great, Mom. Thanks, really. I just hope I don't lose it."

"Please don't. I don't want to have to go back to Japan to get you another one."

Something about that didn't sound right. "Does that mean you are going back?"

"No," she said, and started to say something else, but was interrupted when the waitress reappeared with our food.

"You didn't answer my question before about Grandpa. And don't give me that 'I'm not a doctor' routine. I know you're not a doctor, but you're not stupid, either."

"Well then, I'd say he's not good at all. He's lost weight, he's coughing up blood and he's barely getting around. That's from the chemo, I think, but still . . .."

"Okay, so not so good," she said, and I could tell she was thinking. "I remember you said you had a surprise for me. Please don't tell me you're getting married to this Mary Alice girl."

"Nothing like that." I took out my wallet and showed her my Kansas driver's license. "Grandpa taught me. He needed help getting back and forth to the treatment center in Wichita."

I thought she might have a problem with me having a license, but she just nodded. "Well, that's one less thing we'll have to worry about."

"What do you mean?"

"Connor, while I was in Japan, I made quite a few phone calls. I talked to Dr. Morrow, in Wichita. And I'm sorry to have to tell you this, but he doesn't think the treatments your grandfather has been getting are doing any good. He said the cancer has spread, and that there doesn't seem to be any reason to continue the chemo. He also doesn't think radiation will help very much. At this point, he's recommending palliative care. That means, just medication to provide pain relief and keep him as comfortable as possible."

"Wait, is he saying Grandpa's going to die?"

Mom nodded slowly. "Doctor Morrow thinks maybe six months, maybe not even that long."

"Mom," I began.

She reached across the table and covered my hand with hers. "Let me finish. I told you I had another surprise for you."

"Dad's coming home?"

"No, I'm afraid we still don't know anything one way or the other."

It was all coming too fast. "Then what?"

"Well," she said, "as I told you I made a lot of phone calls. Some were to Dr. Morrow, in Wichita. The others were to the director of the Sunflower County Hospital. They've offered me a position as an attending physician, and I decided to accept it. I'm starting there the first week in October. I guess like most small towns, doctors in Goldenrod are in short supply."

"But what about the Navy? You can't just quit, can you?"

"Actually, I can. And I did. While I was in Japan, I had a chance to do a lot of thinking. I'm tired of moving around all the time, and you're getting ready to start high school. I think it's important that you have a chance to finish where you start, and for both of us to make some friends that we can hang on to for a while. I also think that I want to be close to my dad—to your grandfather—to help him in whatever way I can for however much time he has left, because he's going to have a hard time. With all that in mind, I resigned my commission. At the end of September, once the paperwork is processed, I'll be a civilian. In the meantime, I'm on extended leave."

I could scarcely believe what I was hearing. "Then what are you saying, that we're moving to Kansas?" I didn't know whether to laugh or cry.

"Depends," she said. "Are you willing to make one more move, this time for good?"

I was more than willing. And as soon as I got back home, before I even got my sea bag out of the car, I got on the phone to Mal.

And this time, I had a story for her.

EPILOGUE

Toward the end of September, Mom and I loaded up our personal belongings and took two days to drive in her car from Fresno, California, to Wichita, Kansas, where we arrived late and spent the night in a Holiday Inn motel. The next day we completed our journey—our journey home—to Goldenrod. Besides Grandpa, Mal and Robbie were there to greet us, along with Louise Porter, Dr. and Mrs. Mueller, Mr. and Mrs. Curtis and even Dennis Smith, who was hobbling around on crutches. After a short "Welcome to Goldenrod" party, Mom and I got moved into Grandpa's house. Mom claimed the second downstairs bedroom, so she could be closer to Grandpa, and I hiked back up the stairs to the second-floor bedroom I had occupied during the summer.

During the month I had been back in California, Grandpa had stopped making the twice-weekly trip to Wichita for his chemo treatments, and actually looked better than he had when I left. He had gained some of his weight back and seemed more energetic, but Mom explained that cancer patients usually experience a short period of remission, where they actually do feel better. Unfortunately, his upturn didn't last, and shortly after Christmas, Grandpa died, not from his cancer, but in his sleep from heart failure. By that time, Mom had been working in the emergency room at the county hospital for a couple of months and had already started thinking about partnering with another doctor to open a practice of their own.

At Grandpa's funeral, it seemed as though everyone in the county turned out to pay their respects, including friends and neighbors, work associates and even a few ex-offenders he had sent to jail at one time or another. Uncle Jonathan came back from Saudi Arabia, where he had been living and working for an oil company and had a happy reunion with Mom. Even newly-elected Senator Robert Dole, who had shared the stage at last year's Fourth of July picnic, and many years later would later run for President, turned up to say a few words. And this time, it didn't sound like a campaign speech.

Before Uncle Jonathan returned to Saudi Arabia, the family got together for the reading of Grandpa's will. It turned out he had quite a bit of money, plus some investments, which were split between Mom and Uncle Jonathan. His house went to Mom, and he left the Cadillac to me, which left me absolutely floored. I would be the only kid at Sunflower County High School who would be driving himself (and Mal, of course) to school every day in a nearly-new Cadillac.

It took a few more years, but the Vietnam War finally ended for the United States on January 29, 1973, the date the Paris Agreement was signed by representatives of North and South Vietnam, the United States and the Provisional Revolutionary Government, a shadow government allied with North Vietnam and operating in the south. The last American combat troops left South Vietnam on March 29, 1973. As part of the January 29 agreement, the government of North Vietnam began releasing American POWs, beginning on February 12. The first to come home was Navy pilot Lieutenant Everett Alvarez, the longest-held POW. He was followed, as the prisoners themselves had previously agreed, by the remaining POWs, in order of their date of capture.

Mom and I did not find out until shortly before his release on March 10, that my father was alive and had been a prisoner in North Vietnam since the day his plane was shot down. His journey home took him from prison to Gia Lam military airport in Hanoi, North Vietnam, to Clark Air Force Base on Luzon Island, in the Philippines, to San Francisco. On the day he arrived, Mom and I were waiting, with tears in our eyes and smiles on our faces, to meet him.